IF SHE DIDN'T GET AWAY INSTANTLY, SHE'D BE LOST . . .

But it was like pushing against a rock wall. His lips softened then, and the steel in his arms melted. His mouth caressed hers. She could have pulled away now, but she didn't. Her arms slipped up over his chest and curled around his neck. Her body arched tightly against his. Though her mind was incapable of thought, every other inch of her knew that this was where she belonged, in his arms and a part of him. The Fourth of July rocket she had feared went off inside of her with an explosion of sparks.

WHAT ARE *LOVESWEPT* ROMANCES?

They are stories of true romance and touching emotion. We believe those two very important ingredients are constants in our highly sensual and very believable stories in the *LOVESWEPT* line. Our goal is to give you, the reader, stories of consistently high quality that may sometimes make you laugh, sometimes make you cry, but are always fresh and creative and contain many delightful surprises within their pages.

Most romance fans read an enormous number of books. Those they truly love, they keep. Others may be traded with friends and soon forgotten. We hope that each *LOVESWEPT* romance will be a treasure—a "keeper." We will always try to publish

*LOVE STORIES YOU'LL NEVER FORGET
BY AUTHORS YOU'LL ALWAYS REMEMBER*

The Editors

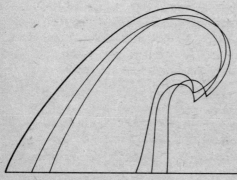

LOVESWEPT • 12

Joan J. Domning
Hunter's Payne

BANTAM BOOKS · TORONTO · NEW YORK · LONDON · SYDNEY

HUNTER'S PAYNE

A Bantam Book / July 1983

*LOVESWEPT and the wave device are trademarks of
Bantam Books, Inc.*

ISBN 0-553-21611-2

Published simultaneously in the United States and Canada

---

*Bantam Books are published by Bantam Books, Inc.
Its trademark, consisting of the words "Bantam Books"
and the portrayal of a rooster, is Registered in U.S. Patent
and Trademark Office and in other countries. Marca
Registrada. Bantam Books, Inc., 666 Fifth Avenue, New York,
New York 10103.*

PRINTED IN THE UNITED STATES OF AMERICA

O   0 9 8 7 6 5 4 3 2 1

One

Karen Hunter walked through the sweltering heat of downtown Denver. The windows of the towering buildings on either side of Fifteenth Street glared in the relentless August sunlight. The roaring traffic and random shouts and laughter from the crowd of tourists and native Coloradans on the busy congested street seemed to give the heat wave a voice. Even this early, at eleven in the morning, Karen could smell the heat shimmering up from the asphalt and feel it scorch her feet through the thin soles of her flimsy, high-heeled sandals.

The revolving door of one of the huge buildings swept her mercifully into its air-conditioned lobby. She waited for a moment until her eyes adjusted to the dim lighting, then studied the directory until she touched the name she was looking for with one slim finger. P. Lee Payne & Associates,

Photography. It seemed an insignificant title for what she hoped would be her big chance.

Before she took the elevator, Karen stopped in the rest room to peer at herself in the mirror. It was important that she look capable, professional and mature. What she saw instead were a couple of worried, honey-brown eyes, wheat-blond hair slipping away from the smooth twist at the back of her head to crimp into moist baby curls in the perspiration on her forehead, and cheeks broiled ruddy as a child's from the sun. Her brand-new gray shantung suit had wilted in the heat.

"Damn," she murmured. She was struggling to make a place for herself in a business where maturity and poise were imperative, and even at her best she looked younger than her twenty-six years. Her tilted eyes and brows over high cheekbones and a pointed chin gave her a kittenish look rather than an image that might command respect. She couldn't even claim beauty. Cute, that's what she was. "Damn," she snorted again.

Karen worked for the *New Colorado Review*, a floundering local magazine that specialized in reporting the entertainment, art and recreational news in and around Denver. Her position was assistant to the editor, which meant she was a glorified secretary and all around gofer.

Not that she was complaining, because there were thousands of journalism graduates who would kill for the chance to be connected in any way with any publication. But she wanted more; she wanted to write her own copy under her own by-line, for something bigger and more important, the *Denver Post*, for example.

P. Lee Payne could open the door to that possibility. He was *the* leading photographer in the area, one of the top ten in the country, and quickly achieving international fame. And he had never granted an interview—not because journalists didn't try. He was besieged by the press.

Karen had pleaded with her boss for the time away from the office to try to see the great P. Lee Payne. When Dan Benedict had finally grudgingly agreed—to get her out of his hair, she suspected— he had laughed and asked, "What makes you think a young woman like you can succeed where your elders and betters have failed?" She was determined to show him, and to prove herself. If she could get this interview, she knew she'd be allowed to handle other assignments; then her career would bound ahead . . . to a beginning. She had to prove that all those years of struggling to get a college education were worth the effort.

The elevator whispered open to let her on and whispered shut after her. She pressed the button marked sixteen, and watched the numbers flip above the door. What would P. Lee Payne be like? An older man, she imagined, dignified, with gray hair, suave. She had never seen him and knew very little about him beyond the fact that he was important in the worlds of photography and art.

A set of double glass doors immediately across from the elevator bore the gold-lettered legend, "P. Lee Payne & Associates, Photography." Karen's heart thumped like the feet of a frightened rabbit. Could she pull it off? She had to. With a tug at her skirt and a careful pat on the white lace at her throat, she opened the door and stepped into the reception room of the studio.

Everything oozed subdued elegance, the thick, spongy azure carpeting under her feet, the stark off-white walls decorated with groupings of formal portraits intermingled with art shots of ordinary people caught in the grip of extraordinary emotions. Several raw, overpowering oil paintings dominated the room.

Karen gave her attention to the receptionist sitting behind a polished desk, guarding the door into the studio itself. Deborah Horne, the name plaque informed. Deborah graced the room in a long, lean, fashion-model manner, with heavy auburn hair framing a face rich with graceful angles and high cheekbones. She cupped her hand over the telephone receiver at her ear and gave Karen a smile. "If you would care to take a seat, I'll be with you as soon as I can," she said in a low, husky voice. Karen turned away. So that was the kind of woman who appealed to P. Lee Payne. Her confidence began to crumble.

In a secluded ell off the room, there were several comfortable lime-green and navy-blue chairs for clients who might have to wait. Karen walked toward them.

The only other person waiting blocked her entrance with a pair of long legs stretched out in front of him, long legs and a body to match. He was a big man dressed in faded, tight blue jeans with a frayed hole in one knee, and a wrinkled, paint-smeared work shirt with the sleeves rolled up over muscular arms. Considering the worn cowboy boots covering the feet crossed in her path and the battered, flat-crowned felt cowboy hat he had tilted down over his forehead, Karen judged wryly that he had just come in from the corral out back. She wondered what he was doing in a place like this. She couldn't see his eyes under the brim of his hat, but there was just enough glint to let her know he was watching her. She waited for him to move his legs to let her pass. He didn't.

Which left her with the choice of standing in front of the receptionist's desk like a naughty schoolgirl or stepping over his feet. She stepped over the dusty boots and took a seat in a green chair.

His head and attention had followed her, and he wasn't helping her to maintain her composure; there was too much blatant masculinity under those disreputable clothes, the muscles and tan of an active outdoorsman. She wished he would stop watching her, and silently cursed when her purse dropped out of her nervous fingers. She picked it up and glared at the man.

He seemed aware that he was bothering her, and his lips turned up in amusement as he hooked his thumbs in his belt to let his fingers lie lightly on either side of the fly of his tight jeans.

Karen gave another silent curse, as she felt heat rise from her neck to her face, and turned her attention deliberately toward the pictures on the wall.

The receptionist murmured on, giving husky instructions for a future appointment. As the minutes stretched, Karen felt her equilibrium shattering. It wasn't necessary to look at that . . . ranch hand . . . to know that his eyes were traveling up and down her body. She had to force herself not to pull her skirt down over her knees. Her chest was tight with anger.

After an eternity, Deborah hung up the phone and moved gracefully around her desk to stand just on the other side of that pair of long, disturbing legs. "I'm sorry you had to wait," she said, smiling at Karen. "How may I help you?" Her cool, unruffled exterior led Karen to believe that this young woman would never let a trifling thing like a sensual man disturb her calm.

Karen stood up, hating having to present herself over the man in the chair. "I'd like to make an appointment to have my portrait done by Mr. Payne," she said. "As soon as possible. It's rather important." Very important, she thought. If she could get him alone, a captive audience, she could convince him to let her interview him.

"Oh," Deborah said, looking sympathetic, "I'm afraid we're booked solid until next April; then one of Mr. Payne's associates could fit you in."

Karen's heart sank. "But I had particularly wanted Mr. Payne to do me." She hesitated, then added, "I'm a personal friend of his. We knew each other years ago, and I'm sure he'd want to do my picture for me." Her little lie seemed necessary.

Deborah hesitated for at least five seconds. There was a fleeting, strangely distressed look on her flawless face. "Mr. Payne very seldom does any actual shooting in the studio," she said. "His associates handle that, but if you could leave your name and phone number, I'll give him your message."

This wasn't going the way Karen had planned. She glanced angrily at the man in the chair. The smile on his face had widened. He was enjoying her discomfort. If he hadn't been there, disturbing every nerve in her body, she could have thought of some way to get around this dilemma. At least she didn't have to continue the conversation over his legs and tight pants. She walked toward Deborah, stepping over his boots, deliberately letting one toe kick his ankle. The grin on his face made a bright white flash in the tan of his face. She hated him.

At the desk, Karen wrote her name on a piece of paper, and jotted her office number. The call would come directly to her desk, rather than go through the switchboard at the *Review*. She didn't want Payne to know she worked for a publication until she had him softened up. If he had any curiosity about his "old friend," he would call her there, she hoped. "Tell him I'll be waiting for his call," she said, handing the paper to Deborah. "It's been so many years, maybe he won't remember me, but it'll be fun to talk over old times." She gave her friendliest smile and turned to leave.

As she walked toward the door, she glanced at the ranch hand. Her knees turned to water and wobbled. He had pulled himself up in the chair, his elbows on his knees. With his hat pushed back, he looked at her with a pair of eyes like ripe olives under a Mediterranean sun. She'd never seen eyes like that, and they made each fiber in her body twitch as if it had been jolted by an electrical shock.

She didn't breathe until she was safely in the elevator. It almost seemed that he had meant to follow her. She huffed a sigh of relief that he hadn't . . . and swallowed a bitter taste of disappointment.

Out in the brutal sunlight on Fifteenth Street, Karen put the intriguing ranch hand out of her mind and concentrated on how she would present herself if P. Lee Payne had enough curiosity to call her. It would take finesse to talk him into an interview.

As Karen drove her yellow Volkswagen west on Colfax Avenue back toward Lakewood, the western suburb of Denver where the *Review* was located, she watched the mountains silhouetted against the blue sky in the distance. They looked gray and cool and protective. The metal roof of the car radiated heat down on her head, and she could think of nothing more appealing than to drive on past Lakewood and keep going up the winding highway to the hills. The higher altitude and the cool, piney air would certainly be easier to face than Dan Benedict, who wouldn't hesitate to remind her that her scheme to meet P. Lee Payne was harebrained and doomed to failure.

The offices of the *New Colorado Review* huddled on a back street of downtown Lakewood, struggling to keep up their appearances, just as the magazine was. Karen walked in the front door, past the front desk, with a nod to the girl behind the counter, and hurried through the main room, with its clatter of typewriters and idle conversation, toward her office in the back.

The only person who noticed her was Hank Mitchell, a sandy-haired man with a sweet smile and flashing dimples, who, when he wasn't pursuing Karen, wrote most of the copy for the *Review*. He threw her a kiss as she disappeared into her office in the back of the building. It was impossible not to compare Hank to that damned, seductive cowboy in the studio, and poor Hank paled dismally.

Karen shrugged off her suit jacket, hung it over the back of her chair and sat down to look around the minuscule, stuffy little office. The walls were drab, her desk was scarred and cluttered with busy work, and the room was barely big enough to hold the desk, a couple of chairs and a bank of filing cabinets. She picked up a crystal paperweight and turned it slowly, watching the light reflect rainbows through its convoluted inner core. Her life didn't have room for a relationship, not even a nice, friendly, safe one with Hank, until she could prove that she could live up to her father's example. Yet she couldn't stop the turbulence and itch inspired by those dark eyes of the cowboy. Putting the paperweight down, she stretched to pull her damp, silky blouse away from her perspiring back. The smooth material clung to her breasts, and the sensation brought the image of the cowboy's broad shoulders back into full focus in her mind. She wondered dreamily what it might be like to have her breasts pressed against that chest.

Then she dropped her arms angrily. That man had been annoying, irritating, inconsiderate, egotistical. She turned to the paperwork on her desk. A sloppy, presumptuous man—and he had been laughing at her because she couldn't ignore him. Thank goodness she'd never see him again.

By the time Karen had answered ten letters from disgruntled readers and had made eight calls to nightclubs around the area to inquire about up-and-coming entertainment, she had passed beyond ladylike perspiration to being sweaty and her stomach complained, reminding her that she had forgotten to eat lunch. The second hand of the clock on the wall ticked too slowly, and it was only four-fifteen, leaving another three-quarters of an hour before she could go home to a cool—no, a cold—shower and something tall and icy to drink.

With a sigh, she dabbed the wet beads on her upper lip with a fingertip, and unbuttoned one more button on her blouse. Then she got up to file the copies of the letters she had written in the filing cabinet in the corner.

Before she had finished, Dan Benedict appeared in her open door, startling her. She frowned and opened her mouth to protest that she was in no mood to hear any of his smart remarks about her P. Lee Payne scheme. She looked at him and didn't speak. He was a heavy, shaggy man in his sixties, and at this particular moment, he was standing straighter than she had ever seen him. His face held a stunned expression that killed any flip remark she might have planned to make.

Before she could ask what the problem was, he said, "Here's someone to see you, Karen." He stood aside for her visitor to enter, then withdrew, without another word, to close the door.

Karen closed her eyes briefly, every bit of her embarrassment surging up to remind her of that miserable encounter in the studio, downtown. She opened her eyes and clutched the edge of the filing drawer with white knuckles. "What are *you* doing here?" she demanded angrily. "Did you follow me?" All she needed was trouble from someone like him.

The ranch hand was too big for her little office; he crowded it uncomfortably. The man himself didn't match either the grubby office or his shabby clothes. He was as devastating in her little cubbyhole as he had been in the glamorous downtown studio. His cowboy hat was set square across his forehead, and those bottomless dark eyes bored into Karen's angry brown ones.

"Hello to you, too, Ms. Karen Hunter." His voice

was as deep as his chest and sent a chill up Karen's spine. "No, I didn't follow you; I picked up the phone, and the telephone company was nice enough to give me the address for this number." She looked blank. He smiled slightly, not a terribly friendly smile. "You left your name and number with P. Lee Payne's receptionist, remember?"

How could she forget? She was not proud of her performance in front of the glamorous Deborah Horne and this, this . . . louse. "That certainly wasn't for your benefit. What do you want, anyway?" she snapped.

He stuck his hands in his back pockets and looked around the room lazily; then he hunched his shoulders and let them drop. "You sure keep it hot in here."

"So leave, then," Karen said.

He didn't acknowledge her rudeness. "So you work for a newspaper? You a reporter?"

"It's not a newspaper, it's a magazine, and no, I'm not a reporter, I'm an assistant to the editor, if it's any of your business." She held the letters in her hand stiffly in front of her chest as a fruitless barrier against his eyes.

He ambled toward her, trapping her in the corner with the filing cabinet, and stopped a couple steps away from her. "You don't care much for me, do you?" Those dark eyes under the hat were laughing at her.

At five feet and a little less than five inches, she looked straight ahead at his collarbones and at the tiny pulse that beat between them. He was well over six feet tall. When she looked up into his face, she had the annoying feeling that it looked as if she were turning her head up for a kiss. A kiss . . . She dropped the letters in the drawer and escaped from her corner to sit in the swivel chair at her desk. It was the safest position in the room.

"I don't care one way or another about you. Why should I? I don't even know you. All I know is that you were making fun of me back in that studio and I didn't like it."

He took his hands out of his back pockets and sat on the front edge of her desk. There was a key ring with several keys in his hand, and he tossed it in the air a couple of times, watching it fall, catching it deftly. "You aren't an old friend of P. Lee Payne's. You've never met him."

Karen felt an incriminating blush creep up her neck. She leaned back in her swivel chair and rocked angrily. "How would you know whether I have or haven't?"

"Because you can't lie worth a damn. Guilt is smeared all over your face like jam. Besides, I got it straight from him that he'd never heard of you."

She sat up. "Straight from him?" Her brow furrowed as she thought for a second. "What are you, then, his bodyguard?" It was possible. He was big and strong enough, in his prime at maybe thirty-three or -four; and despite his sloppy garb, he looked intelligent. For an instant, she wondered if she could get to Mr. Payne through him. That idea died as soon as it was conceived. No one would be stupid enough to try to manipulate this man.

"Bodyguard? Let's just say I look out for P. Lee Payne's interests," he said with a nasty little smile. He put down the keys he had been holding and picked up the crystal paperweight to look into its depth, then tossed it in the air and caught it. "What's your interest in P. Lee Payne?"

Karen watched the paperweight, then she caught it herself on the next toss and put it firmly on the desk. "It's valuable," she said, "it belonged to my father. I don't want it broken." She decided to use honesty. "I'd like to interview Mr. Payne. He has never had a personality sketch printed, and the public is interested in people of his stature. They like to read about how other people become successful, where they came from, what they dream about, about their families and their home life. He's such a private person that he encourages curiosity."

The man on the edge of her desk leaned in toward her face. "An interview for you to write up, especially about someone like P. Lee Payne, would get you out of this hot little office, wouldn't it? Send you right on to bigger and better things?"

Karen leaned back, away from him. "Is that bad?" she asked under his piercing look.

He leaned closer. "P. Lee Payne does not like to be hassled by the kind of extortionist who would come into his studio and claim to know him. He is indeed a private person, and he has that right." He leaned further in, and Karen shrank in her chair. His finger spindled the middle of the bare spot on her chest where the blouse was unbuttoned. "Don't try anything like that again. You leave him alone."

For a few seconds, she was paralyzed by the finger and the threatening tone in his voice, and stared up at him with wide eyes. Then she slapped his finger away and sat up straight. "And if I don't, is it your job to take me into some dark alley and beat me up? You're twice as big as I am, so that should make you proud." She'd be damned if she'd let him see how badly he had frightened her. Besides, all she had to do was scream once and at least four people would be in her office in a flash.

His dark eyes lost their threat, and he grinned. "I could think of better things to do with you in a dark alley." His eyes brushed the damp silk of her blouse clinging to her breasts.

Karen jumped up, sending her chair rolling back. "You get out of here, you egotistical slob." He didn't move, and she began to shake with anger. "You've delivered your message. That's what you came for, isn't it? Now, get out, and don't you ever, ever come back here."

He looked at her speculatively for a minute; then he tapped his hat further down over his eyes and left. Karen stared after him, thinking: of all the presumptuous, overbearing . . .

Then she took a deep breath and sat down. So much for P. Lee Payne. He'd get a fine report back about her. She dropped her head in disappointment. The ranch hand's keys lay on her desk, where he had forgotten them. "Damn," she said. "Damn, damn, damn!" She threw the keys in her drawer and slammed it shut.

Five minutes later, when Dan Benedict poked his head through the door, Karen had her chin propped on both fists as she sat behind her desk sulking. He grinned happily and walked in to stand like a disheveled bear in front of her. "How did you do it?" he asked in his gravelly voice. "Here I've been laughing at you, and you've gone ahead and done what no one else could do. I've got to hand it to you. How did you manage? What kind of magic did you use?" His eyes beamed at her from under his bushy eyebrows.

Karen looked up at him, puzzled, her chin still on her fists. "How'd I do what?"

He raised his eyebrows. "Get P. Lee Payne right here into this building, right into this room with you. What else?"

Karen stared at him blankly. "What are you talking about?" Her fists dropped, and she stiffened her shoulders slightly under the weight of her suspicion.

Dan stared back at her, then he lowered his brows. "You mean you didn't know that was Payne here, visiting you? How could you not know?"

"You saw him. He looked like a bum," she said defensively. "I thought he was a bodyguard. I thought . . ." Her fists ground into her forehead, and she squeezed her eyes shut in realization of her stupidity.

Dan reached out and patted her on the head. "He was probably checking you out. Don't worry. This is the closest he's ever come to letting one of our kind talk to him. He'll be back."

Opening her eyes, Karen pushed her fists back over her ears so she wouldn't have to hear his reaction when she said, "I don't think so. I kicked him out. I told him to never, never come back."

Dan glowered at her in amazement. Then he turned his back, shoved his hands in his pants pockets and stared out of the cloudy, dirty window. Finally he turned around and glared at Karen with steely eyes. "I didn't hear what you just said, young lady," he growled, "but if you don't straighten out this gross imbecility and smooth things over with Payne, I am going to fire you. All we need right now, with all of our other problems, is to have one of my staff insult P. Lee Payne."

Karen put her palms on her cheeks to support

her miserable head. "You don't have to fire me," she said, "I'm making plans to jump off a cliff."

"Good!" Dan said sharply, walking to the door, "but first you apologize to Payne." He stalked out, leaving the door open so anyone who might be passing could glance in and see Karen's humiliation.

The seconds ticked off on the clock on the wall. Karen didn't move. Her elbows hurt from pressing on her desk. Her head ached, and her body had cramped after half an hour of silent, motionless self-castigation. She could hear the people in the other rooms closing up shop and getting ready to leave. She felt abandoned and hopeless. She had no doubt that Dan meant what he said, and she'd never get another chance to work for any kind of publication if she lost this job. "Fool," she muttered. It seemed so obvious now; why couldn't she have seen it when P. Lee Payne himself had been in front of her? Because all she had seen was a big hulk of delicious man, and she'd been too busy trying to prove it hadn't affected every gland in her body, that was why. She stared at the paperweight dismally. The great P. Lee Payne wouldn't let her get within a mile of him, after the way she'd treated him. She might as well kiss this dingy little office good-bye.

Finally, she lifted her head and stood up. And sat down abruptly. The great P. Lee Payne lounged in her doorway, watching her. She opened her mouth, but for the life of her, she couldn't think of a word to say.

He pushed away from the door frame with a shoulder and walked to her desk to take his place on the edge. "I take it, from the expression on your face, that the secret is out." He grinned.

"Don't ever try to con anyone again; you're as transparent as this piece of glass." He held up the paperweight, then put it down again carefully.

At the sound of his voice, the frozen gears in Karen's brain began to move. She considered how to present herself, after the way she had treated him. For some unfathomable reason, she must have intrigued him with her impertinence, so it wouldn't be wise to do an about-face and become ingratiating. Leaning back in her desk chair and rocking slightly, she smiled. "You're a fine one to talk about conning, Mr. Payne. Bodyguard, indeed."

Reaching up, he pushed his hat back on his head with a thumb. Thick, damp black hair lay on his forehead. "I couldn't resist. You're so gullible."

"Made your whole day, did it, that little joke?" Karen squirmed slightly in her chair. She hated being made a fool of. "It wasn't gullible not to recognize you. I didn't dream that P. Lee Payne would come dressed like that, and with a hole in the knee of his pants."

He picked at the frayed threads on the knee bent over the edge of the desk. His fingers were surprisingly slim and sensitive-looking for such a big man. "I've been working, and I had to go into Denver on an errand. It was so hot that I stopped at the studio to cool off for a while in the air conditioning." He looked up and let his dark eyes roam over her. "It's lucky I did or I'd never have known what a cute little 'old friend' I had." Then he laughed. "Don't you waste a lot of energy blushing like that whenever someone looks at you?"

Karen rocked in staccato jerks. "Why did you come back?" she asked.

"You mean after you told me never, ever to show my face around here again?" he asked smugly.

An apology would be pointless, when it was obvious that he hadn't taken her words to heart anyway. "Are you considering, just possibly, letting me do a personal sketch about you?" she asked.

His eyes chilled, and the hat was tapped down abruptly over his forehead. "Not likely, and don't even consider making something out of what little you have now. If you write one word about me, I'll sue your pretty little pants off for invasion of privacy." There wasn't the trace of a smile on his lips. "I came back for my keys. I must have left them on your desk."

Keys. She forced herself not to glance at the desk drawer. If she could wangle just a little more time with him, just enough to let him know he could trust her, there might be that millimeter of a chance that she could talk him into an interview.

"What keys?" she asked, looking around. "I haven't seen them. Maybe you dropped them somewhere else." She rocked slowly, keeping her face bland and innocent. "You can see they aren't on the desk or the floor. There isn't enough space in this office to misplace anything."

He sat silently looking at her, then he thumbed his hat back again. "Well, that's a problem. They aren't between here and the car. I looked. I've got an important meeting in"—he glanced up at the clock; it read five-thirty—"a little less than two hours. How am I going to get home, change and get to the meeting without my car keys?"

He left it wide open for her. "I suppose I can drive you home. You must have an extra set of keys, and we can come back for the car."

"Now, that's very thoughtful of you, Ms. Hunter, ma'am," he drawled, "but home is on the other side of Evergreen, about thirty miles from here. Is the offer still good?"

"Evergreen," she repeated, as if considering it. That was great. Given an hour or so in the car with him, she couldn't help but make a favorable impression on him. "Why not? After sitting here in this heat, a drive in the mountains would be heaven." She smiled. "And my name is Karen." She stood up and picked up her jacket and purse.

He watched her. "Mine is P. Lee Payne, and don't you forget about that dark alley if you have any intention of writing a word about me."

"Yes, sir!" Karen shrugged into her jacket.

"But you can call me Lee if you behave yourself." He followed her out of the office.

Two

The inside of Karen's yellow Volkswagen felt like an oven set on medium heat. The sun had moved down toward the mountains in the west, but its heat waves still radiated off the asphalt parking lot. Gingerly climbing into the car, she held her body away from the vinyl seat and felt the sweat trickle down her back as she reached over to unlock the passenger door. Lee Payne got in, and she started the car.

"Do you have time for me to stop at my house to change clothes?" she asked. "I feel as if I'd been sitting in a sauna all day. I live only a few blocks from here."

"If you make it fast," he answered, glancing at his watch. "My meeting starts at seven-thirty."

Karen parked the car in front of a modest tri-level house in a well-kept neighborhood. She glanced at Lee. There was no way she could justify expecting him to wait in the hot car, even for the few minutes it would take her to change. "Do you want to wait in the house?" she asked. He nodded, and they got out of the car.

It was relatively cool in the house, with the drapes drawn against the sun. The sound of a discordant rumbling came from the lower level of the house. "You can sit there," Karen said, motioning toward the living room. "I'll get my mother, and she'll find you something cool to drink. She's down in her workshop. I can't imagine what she's doing; it sounds like she's tearing the house down."

Karen started down the stairs, and, to her annoyance, Lee followed.

The downstairs room was cluttered with craft debris. Elsie Hunter, a retired schoolteacher, occupied her time doing and teaching crafts—greenware, collage and anything else that took her fancy. Just now, she was bending over a table covered with oily newspapers, a screwdriver in her hand, and her body wrapped in a filthy apron.

"Mom," Karen said, raising her voice over the rattle. "Shut that thing off for a minute."

Elsie didn't raise her head. "I can't get this hellish rock polisher to work right, Karen Jane," she said irritably, poking at the small machine on the table with her screwdriver.

Karen glanced at Lee. He was grinning. "Shut it off," she shouted. "We've got company."

The ear-torturing rattle died away, and Elsie wiped her hands on an oily rag. Karen tossed out a hasty introduction. "Mom, this is Lee Payne. I've got to change. Can you find him something to drink?" She turned without waiting for an answer.

On her way up the stairs, she heard her mother say, "How nice to meet you, Mr. Payne. Karen doesn't often bring anyone home. She's much too solitary, that girl."

Karen turned her eyes to the ceiling. "Oh, God," she muttered, and ran the rest of the way up the second set of stairs to her room.

Hurriedly, she slipped off her suit, blouse and panty hose and rinsed her face and arms with cold water. Then she put on a pair of pale-blue slacks and a white knit top with cap sleeves and a scoop neck. After she'd slipped into a pair of white sandals, she hesitated, then sprayed just a little flowery perfume under each ear and down the front of her top. One glance told her she looked much more in her own element now than when she'd been trying to look sophisticated in her suit.

She ran back downstairs. Lee looked up from the rock polisher, checked her outfit approvingly and protested, "So soon? Your mother has been telling me all about you." He was holding the screwdriver now.

"I thought you were in a hurry," Karen answered stuffily. She wasn't keen on having *him* know about *her*.

Adroitly, then, she maneuvered him out of the house. When Lee suggested that he knew the way and should drive, Karen agreed; she welcomed the opportunity to sit back and watch him. But as it happened, she didn't relax, and she spent more time watching the speedometer than Lee. She couldn't deny his hands were steady on the wheel of the VW and he seemed in complete control, but anything above the proscribed speed limit terrified her.

Once she caught him glancing at her as if he knew that his speeding bothered her. She un-clamped her fingers from around the armrest and folded her hands loosely in her lap, while she tossed around in her mind for a conversational opener.

Before she could think of one, Lee said, "Karen *Jane*, well, well."

"Oh, please, spare me that. No one but my mother calls me Karen Jane."

"Aren't you a little old to be living with your mommie?"

"It's convenient, and I don't see that it's any of your business."

The pressure on the accelerator increased suddenly, and Karen's fingers clawed the armrest. Her eyes darted to the speedometer, then back for a hasty check for the highway patrol, then anxiously at Lee. Grimly, she turned toward the front and watched the signs flash by.

As the altitude increased, the temperature of the air flowing in the open window lowered, cooling and drying Karen's sweaty skin. The evergreen trees lining the road gave off a pungent scent. She sighed deeply.

Several miles beyond Evergreen, Lee turned off onto a two-lane road, then, shortly after that, onto a narrow, winding gravel lane that twisted steeply up through a dense, unpopulated forest. Karen bit her lip nervously. She hadn't expected this much wilderness. She glanced at Lee, and the look on his face led her to believe he knew exactly what she was thinking. At least the narrow road had slowed his speed.

"So you think you'd like to know all about me, do you?" he asked.

Karen was beginning to wish she'd never heard of him. He had his hat pushed down to hide his eyes again. All she could see was a solid, set jaw with its smudge of black beard and a small white scar on the side of his chin. "Ye-e-ss." She dragged the word out, tentatively. "Maybe not everything," she qualified. "Have you decided to let me do a sketch on you?" That he even considered it surprised her, and she held her breath for his answer.

"Let's say I'll agree to think about it, with the scales balanced toward no. Does that satisfy you?" He didn't look pleased about it, and he had slowed the car almost to a crawl.

"It's certainly better than a flat-out no."

"Tell me exactly why you want this so badly." He gave her a sharp look and no smile. "And no fabricating."

She winced, then took a deep breath. "I'm working for a moribund monthly publication, doing a dead-end job. I spent six years, off and on, in college working my tail off to try to get a good, solid background for writing and investigative reporting. But I can't break into the media unless I've written something and had it published. Not just written something, but something unique enough to catch the editor's eye and capture readers' imaginations. When you realize there are masses of promising writers and reporters, you can see that an article that is as different as, say, a personality sketch on someone as elusive as P. Lee Payne is a windfall, the wedge in the door." She hesitated, and decided complete honesty was extremely important. "My father was Evan B. Hunter; perhaps you've heard of him. He was one of the greats in news coverage. He died twenty years ago." She swallowed a lump. "We were close. I know I can't hope for the kind of stature and recognition he had, but I'd like to at least be in his field. And that is why I'd like to write about you." She couldn't look at Lee. Instead, she looked out the window at the trees drifting by, with their carpet of rusty, dead pine needles underneath, at the big rough granite boulders on the hillsides. It still hurt her to speak of her father, even after all those years.

For a few minutes, Lee didn't respond; instead, he speeded the car and slewed around a couple of switchbacks, winding the car higher and higher up the hill. Finally, he asked, "Why did it take you so long to get through college? You a little slow up above?"

She didn't know if she should be angry at his flip question after she had bared her soul, or if she felt relieved that he had put the discussion back on an argumentative footing, which was easier to handle. "Not at all. I'm really very smart. But I spent quite a bit of time in hospitals as a kid and got way behind in school. Then, when I went to college, I didn't have enough money to do it all at once. I had to work for a couple of years to save up the tuition. My father might have been famous, but he wasn't very logical, financially speaking."

Lee turned off the gravel road and drove up a long driveway. He stopped the car in front of a fence that shut in a huge, elegantly rustic, A-frame house set against the hillside. He sat thinking, his hands on the wheel. Then he looked at her seriously. "When you start examining another person's life, it's easy to dig up things that are best forgotten."

For a moment, Karen thought he was talking about her life, but it was his own he was thinking of. "I don't need to know your whole life history," she said, "just a few interesting facts, like how you built your business, what you do for fun, about your wife and children." She hesitated; she hadn't considered that he might be married. He didn't reply. "A description of this house would help. Lord, this is spectacular."

"And have curiosity seekers gathering round? No, thanks. That's the problem. If you open the door to making my life public, then a couple of dozen blood suckers will start poking around. I don't want that." He opened the door and got out. "Wait there," he said, and pulled himself up into a pine tree next to the locked gate, rustled around in the branches and then, with an athletic swing, dropped himself down to open the gate with a key he had taken from a cache in the tree.

They didn't continue the conversation as he drove the rest of the way up the driveway to the house. Karen got out and looked around. The house was as tall as the pines that surrounded it. Both the house and the land it stood on spoke loudly and clearly of money. She looked up at the front expanse of glass and cedar beams.

A double door in burnt orange with antique-gold fittings yielded to a key that Lee had taken from the tree. He looked back at Karen, reading her face, and grinned like a kid. He pushed his hat back on his head. "What do you think of it? I designed it myself."

"I've never seen anything like it. For as big as it is, it looks like it grew on this mountain, rather than being built here."

"I meant it to look that way." He was obviously pleased with her response, and held the door open for her. "And, Karen," he said as she passed into the wide, flagstoned foyer, "I'm not married and I don't have any children."

She glanced at him, then away to hide her pleased blush.

Hitting the light switches to bring the house to life, Lee motioned Karen down the four steps that led to an enormous living room. Fascinated, she took a step, then stopped short. Two huge German Shepherds seemed to materialize out of nowhere and flanked her, their bodies stiff, the hair standing up rigidly on their shoulders. Both sets of eyes bored into her over muzzles that seemed at least a foot long. Little rumbling warning growls came from their throats. "Lee . . ." she said in a strangled whisper.

"Sorry, I forgot about them." He pushed the dogs back and knelt between them, a hand ruffling each hairy neck. "It's all right, girls," he crooned. "This is Karen Jane, and anyone with a name like that has got to be harmless." The dogs relaxed enough to wag their tails slightly as they pinioned Karen with their brown eyes. "Let them look you over," he said. "They won't hurt you as long as I'm here. They're my security system. If anyone took a notion to break into this house, they'd wish they hadn't."

"I believe you." Karen stood rooted to the step under her feet as the dogs ran cold noses over her body. She couldn't have moved. She could hardly breathe.

"This one is Freak," Lee said, grabbing a handful of skin and fur, shaking the dog playfully. "And the pretty one here is Sally."

"Sally?" She cocked an eye at the beast.

He laughed. "I'll put them out," he said, to her enormous relief.

When he came back, he bounded up a flight of stairs to a large exposed bedroom on a balcony above the living room. "Make yourself at home," he called down to her. "I've got to hustle if I'm going to make that meeting. Look around if you want to."

He disappeared, and Karen heard the sound of a shower from somewhere in the back of the bedroom, and she turned her attention enthusiastically to the house.

The living room extended through the center of the building, its ceiling running up into the steep A-shape of the house. The expansive windows at each end of it brought the mountain and the trees almost inside. Heavy dark beams crossed the ceiling above, and on the far wall a massive native-stone fireplace dominated the room.

The furniture was masculine and opulently comfortable. Karen sat down on a brown leather davenport; rather, it enveloped her like a feather bed. A polished table beside it was dust-free and uncluttered, except for a pair of expensive gold hoop earrings and a silk designer scarf. She smiled slightly over a stab of jealousy she resolutely forced down. She had no business feeling envy. P. Lee Payne was too much man for her.

She got up to walk across the room and look out the window. She could see to the top of the steep hill, with its boulders and scrubby trees. The backyard had been left in its natural state and glowed with purple and yellow wildflowers.

There were several doors off the living room. A couple of them were closed, and she didn't feel comfortable opening them to snoop, as she wanted to. The open ones had to satisfy her curiosity. There were a couple of bedrooms, unused apparently, a kitchen all done up in Spanish tile and gleaming copper, a dining room with heavy Spanish furniture.

The living room was enough to hold Karen's interest for weeks, and she loved walking on the thick, springy carpeting, a tweed shag in rust and cream. The walls were covered with pale burlap, perfect to display the groupings of paintings and Indian art. Several paintings had traditional Indian motifs, beautifully done in earth colors, signed by the artist, Charlie Whitehorse. The name tickled her memory, but she couldn't recapture what she should have known about him.

The shower had stopped overhead, and an electric razor hummed. Karen walked around restlessly, trying to ignore the sound. She studied a bookcase. About half of the books dealt with art and photography; the rest were a mixture of popular fiction and college textbooks, heavy on psychology. She wondered how she ever could have imagined P. Lee Payne to be a simple ranch hand. She smiled; her hormones must have dimmed her vision when she first saw him. The razor hummed on.

Then it stopped, and the sound of Lee's voice interrupted her thoughts. "I forgot to tell you to have a drink. The liquor's in the cabinet in the corner; the ice cubes and mix are behind the doors under it in the fridge. Help yourself."

Karen turned to look up at him, and felt that miserable blush creep up her cheeks again. He stood leaning against the railing of the balcony, naked and damp from the shower, with a towel wrapped around his middle. Dark hair curled over his chest, tapering into a line that disappeared under the towel. Every muscle knew its place and hugged his body, and those long legs were well shaped and fuzzed with dark hair. He glowed with health and sensuality. Karen glowed right back. She turned away quickly when she realized he had a malicious grin on his handsome face and his Mediterranean eyes were inviting anything she cared to give.

The liquor cabinet took on considerably more interest than she usually felt for drinking as she listened to him opening closet doors and rattling hangers. She splashed a finger of vodka in a glass and filled it with orange juice.

A painting above the cabinet caught her attention. It seemed to be a mass of strident, disorganized color in dots and splotches. She couldn't see the point of it.

"Back away from it," came Lee's voice from overhead. Obviously, he didn't have the qualms about watching her that she did about looking at him.

Obediently backing away, she watched with fascination as, with distance, forms began to take shape in the picture. Materializing out of the jumble of color, the harsh blues and greens over underlying red and ocher, were two children, an odd, pathetic pair, playing in the shallow water at the edge of a lake. No feature of the painting was sharp or clear; it gave only impressions. The children bothered her; the artist hadn't given them a childlike quality. They seemed prematurely aged adults masquerading as children.

Karen moved forward again, watching the clarity of the picture disassemble itself into color, then she backed away and watched the children take form. It wasn't until she had put quite some distance between her eyes and the painting that they began to look childlike. She backed slowly away, frowning.

She hadn't realized Lee had come downstairs until she backed into him. She stiffened convulsively as she felt his strong arms wrap themselves around her from behind. The warmth of his hands burned through the material of her light knit top. Her entire back responded to the feeling of his body against her. She didn't want this, not now. Maybe someday, when she had her life in order . . . She had to get away from him.

He towered over her; she could feel his head bend and his breath on her hair. She knew that if it turned into a wrestling match, she didn't have a prayer of winning, and she wasn't sure she wanted to. She stiffened deliberately. "Not interested, Payne," she said breathlessly. She knew he could feel the jackhammer beat of her heart under the hand he had tucked just under her left breast. The clean scent of soap and shaving lotion was distressingly seductive.

He bent and nuzzled her neck with his lips. Showers of tiny shocks flew over her shoulders. Then he laughed, a soft tantalizing sound, and released her. "Just checking, Hunter."

Karen put a couple of quick steps of safety between them, cursing her hot face, and looked at him. He grinned a challenge. She declined to accept and shook her head slightly. She looked him over—his white dinner jacket complete with black tie and ruffles. Without the hat, his hair was obviously styled, not cut, very dark, just bordering on being curly. "That must be some meeting."

"Some meeting," he agreed, cheerfully. "You head for the door, and I'll let the dogs in."

Karen beat a hasty retreat to the car and climbed

in. She had to smile as he walked toward her. The toes of highly polished black cowboy boots peeped from beneath the cuff of his black trousers.

The ride back to Lakewood was fast and silent. Karen knew that she couldn't say anything that would convince him to let her write about him. He'd have to make that decision himself, with no further distraction. She wasn't certain she felt capable of coping with a man like Lee. If she wasn't careful, she'd tumble like a landslide and get hurt again; she'd done that once and she hadn't liked it. But, oh, she wanted that interview.

Glancing sidelong at Lee, Karen wondered why he had encouraged her interest. It was certainly out of character for him to have anything to do with a journalist. And she certainly wasn't the high-powered type of woman who would appeal to a handsome, successful man like him. She couldn't begin to understand what motivated him.

When Lee finally parked the VW in the parking lot behind the *Review*, beside a blue Blazer that dwarfed the little yellow car, Karen asked, "Have you made up your mind, Payne?"

He got out and leaned down to look in the window at her. "You'll be the first to know when I do, Hunter. Thanks for the ride."

She watched him get in his Blazer and leave, then she blew a puff of air up over her face, as if she had just survived an ordeal. . . .

Three

At eight forty-five the next morning, the only positive thing Karen could think about the day was that it was Friday and the next two days would be her own. She climbed out of her car, which she parked in the back lot of the *Review*, straightened the blue skirt she wore and smoothed the matching blue flowered organza blouse.

She hadn't been seated five minutes when Dan Benedict stalked into her office. "Well?" he inquired. It wasn't necessary for him to elaborate. Karen knew perfectly well what he had on his mind.

She smiled. "Don't worry. The great Payne isn't mad at us—me; he came back, and we're on speaking terms."

"Is he going to give you the interview?" Dan asked. "I suppose you know how much that would mean to this rag."

She did; they would be lucky if they didn't fold in six months. "I wish I could give you a solid yes. The best I could do was to get him to promise to think about it, but he'll probably say no."

Dan opened the door and looked back. "Go to bed with him if you have to, but get that interview."

"Now, wait a minute . . ." she protested, but he had left.

"Go to bed with who?" Hank Mitchell poked his head in the open door with a big, dimpled smile. "Me, I hope."

She threw a pencil at him, and he went on his way with a laugh.

By three o'clock, the heat was oppressive. Karen had finished reading three unsolicited manuscripts that weren't right for the magazine, and she was well into one about the art center in Santa Fe, New Mexico. Many of the Denver artists made their best sales down there. It might do.

The article told of Charlie Whitehorse, a well-known Navaho painter, a celebrity in the art world of Santa Fe, who planned to exhibit at a gallery in Denver next month. Remembering his paintings in Lee's house, she looked up thoughtfully.

Lee stood in her doorway, one shoulder against the frame, watching her.

"Do you always pop up when you're least expected?" she asked. She had convinced herself that it wasn't possible he'd contact her again.

"Whenever I can manage it," he answered. "It's not much fun being predictable." He ambled into the room and sat on her desk. His hat was pushed back, and he looked mischievous.

"What can I do for you?" she asked, leaning back in her chair.

"I thought I'd check to see if you were ready to give my keys back yet."

Oh, lord, she'd forgotten about those damned keys. She sat up straight. "Keys?" she repeated weakly.

He started to reach for the paperweight, then glanced at Karen and jammed his hands in his pockets instead. "Keys. I left them on your desk yesterday on purpose, so I know you've got them."

Karen squirmed. "Why would you leave them on purpose?"

"Why'd you hide them?" He grinned. "So you could take a ride with me?"

She'd never met anyone who could so consistently put her at a disadvantage. She reached in her drawer and angrily threw the keys on the desk.

He stood up and put the keys in his pocket. "Get your purse and let's go," he said, walking to the door to wait for her.

"Go where? I'm not going anywhere with you. I'm working. Some people have to work for a living, you know." Rationally, she knew she should have leaped at the chance to go with him. Had he decided about the interview? But irrationally, she was annoyed, and she wasn't going to be pushed.

"I thought you wanted your picture taken. Seems like it was terribly important yesterday. So I'm going to take your picture."

"I don't want my picture taken. I can't afford you," she said.

"Free of charge," he said, smiling at her little display of irritation. "You can't turn that down."

"I'll bet I can," she said, sitting stubbornly behind her desk.

"You owe it to me. It's been damned inconvenient doing without my keys."

Karen realized that the background noise of voices and typewriters had stilled. She could imagine every head turned to watch and listen and wonder. "Oh, all right," she said and got up to find her purse. "Why do you want to take my picture? And don't try to flatter me that I'm model material."

He walked over to stand close in front of her. "You aren't that, no way. Thank goodness," he said and reached up to cup her face in his two hands, his deep, dark eyes caressing her features. "Too fresh, too cute, too simple." His face came down and his lips touched hers in a tingling graze.

"Lee!" she said warningly in a voice turned husky with the sensations his touch had set in motion.

Grinning impishly, he stepped back, only to let his hands drift down outlining her breasts and waist before they dropped. "Too much breast and hip, too sharp a curve at the waist. You'd have to be flat to be a model. I like you better this way."

"Payne! If this is the way it's going to be—" Her breath came hot and heavy now, each area of her body mentioned burned with the afterglow of his touch.

Retreating to the door, he smiled contritely. "Don't worry, you're safe. I only want to take your picture out of simple curiosity. I'd like to know what's behind your facade."

"What you see and what I've said is all there is," she said, struggling to control the pulse and gasp of desire he had set in motion. "I'm not devious."

"Then why did you keep my keys?" That maddening grin again.

"Oh, those stupid keys," Karen snorted and walked past him.

When they left the building, he helped her into his blue Blazer and they headed toward Denver.

It wasn't until Karen walked into the big building in downtown Denver that she realized how out of place she looked in her casual skirt and blouse, with a pair of leather clogs on her bare feet. She glanced at Lee and felt better. He didn't seem uncomfortable in his work clothes, dressed the same as he had been yesterday, except for a few more stains on his shirt and a different pair of jeans without a hole in the knee.

Deborah, the receptionist, as lovely and sophisticated as Karen remembered, rose to greet them— Lee warmly, and Karen with a cold, speculative look on her face. Her eyes ran disdainfully over Karen's body. Karen wondered if she owned the gold earrings left on the table in Lee's house.

The room beyond the desk to which Lee led Karen was fairly large, but quite dark except for a trio of spotlights trained on a bench set against a drape of velvety aquamarine blue. She could make out three cameras and a maze of wiring on the floor. Mellow music floated out of the darkness.

Lee threw his hat on a chair by the door and said, "Sit down on the bench."

"Now, wait a minute," she protested, "aren't you going to let me comb my hair? I've had a busy day. I must look like the devil."

"Oh, first you don't want your picture taken, and now vanity raises its ugly head." He laughed softly. "Sit down. If you need fixing, I'll fix you."

Karen sighed and sat down. The spotlights blinded her. Lee studied her dispassionately, and she stared back defiantly. Suddenly, he reached toward her and squeaked a baby's rubber toy at her. She laughed, taken by surprise.

"Now that we know the level of your humor," he said, straight-faced, "maybe we can get on with this."

Taking a case out of a closet, he opened it on the floor beside her. It was jammed with clean hair brushes, combs and an assortment of cosmetics. Karen started to object, then thought better of it. Let him have his way, do what he wanted and get it over with. He undid the leather clasp that held her hair, allowing it to cascade over her shoulders. She closed her eyes with the pleasure of feeling his fingers in her hair, the brush making it silky. He cleaned her face with a lemony-smelling wipe and smoothed, dusted and touched it as if he were making a work of art. The electric shocks were working at her body again, and she felt her blood race. "Lick your lips," he said. She did, self-consciously.

Finally, he stood back, and she opened her eyes. When she tried to speak, he shushed her softly, turning her head to suit some vision he imagined. In the position in which he placed her, she had to look straight ahead at the fly of his jeans. The image of him wearing only a towel crept back into her memory. For a second, she speculated what it might be like to . . . Her lips parted breathlessly.

With a restless annoyed movement, Karen broke her pose and looked at his face. He had been studying her seriously, and she hoped he couldn't read her mind.

Moving her on the bench to face the other direction, Lee sat on his heels a little distance from her. At least he had his face on a level with her eyes this time, and far enough away for comfort. Karen began to relax as the soft music floated seductively around her.

"Your mother is a nice lady," he said softly, surprising her. "We fixed the rock polisher this morning."

A spasm of annoyance grabbed at Karen. All she wanted was an interview, and this man was infiltrating her life. She shrugged at a tensing muscle.

After a few minutes of silence, he asked gently, "What happened to your father?"

"A car accident," she answered uncomfortably. Lee seemed to have her mesmerized by the pull of his dark eyes in the circle of light around her.

"Was that why you were hospitalized when you were a child? Were you in the accident with him?"

She nodded mutely.

"You loved him?"

There was a look of sympathy on his dark face; the lines etched around his mouth seemed a reflection of her own painful memory. "He was a beautiful man," she whispered.

She felt as if she had been tried and convicted under the spotlights. She had to get away. "Will you take your pictures and get this over with?" she asked. "I'm tired, and I want to go home."

Lee stood up at once, reaching down to rub a thigh muscle stiff from squatting on his heels. "As a matter of fact, we've taken several different shots already, and if that's all the spirit will allow, then we're done."

She looked at him suspiciously. "But you haven't been near your cameras."

"Meet my associate, Herb Butler." Lee nodded into the darkness of the room. "You were so fascinated with my charming self, you didn't notice him, did you?" He looked pleased with himself.

Karen shaded her eyes from the spotlight and peered into the room to smile uncertainly at the shadowy figure who waved a hand at her from one of the cameras. "Oh, brother," she whispered. She didn't care to speculate about when he might have caught her.

Lee held out her purse and hair clip, then hustled her out of the studio. He didn't speak during the drive back to Lakewood, and Karen was content to sulk in her corner of the Blazer. When he parked in front of her house, she remembered what she was supposed to be doing, and started to ask, "About the interview—"

"I'll let you know," he said abruptly, and reached across her to open her door. It was apparent he couldn't wait to get rid of her.

She stood on the sidewalk, watching the big blue Blazer disappear down the street, trying to make sense out of what had happened. It was impossible to understand the man.

Presently, she remembered irritably that her own car was still in the parking lot behind the *Review*. She'd have to walk to pick it up. But that would have to wait until tomorrow morning. She felt completely drained. Exhausted.

Four

The next morning Karen sat at the kitchen table in an old blue housecoat, sipping a second cup of coffee, reading the front page of the *Denver Post*, happy that it was Saturday, with all of her problems shelved until Monday morning.

Elsie sat across from her poring over the Living and Arts section of the paper. "Here's a picture of your young man," she said, holding up the page, her eyes curious behind her glasses.

Karen peered at the picture. It was Lee in his dinner clothes. "Mom, he is not my young man. I'm hoping to get an interview with him. That's all there is to it."

Elsie smiled and nodded. Karen took the paper away from her and read the item. Lee had presented an award to the most promising student photographer from the University of Colorado. She studied the picture. The student looked dazed and exalted. Lee seemed faintly suspicious of the camera, as if he didn't belong on that side of it, but nevertheless he looked quite handsome and important. She studied his face, with its strong, high-bridged nose, the mouth, with its full lower lip and stubborn line, those dark, dark eyes under curved inquiring brows, his waving hair.

It could be interesting if he were her "young man"—except for the ravishing creature at his side with her hand possessively on his arm, gazing confidently into the lens. The woman, only a few inches shorter than Lee, was as slim as a wand with high, sculptured breasts that showed just a hint of nipple through the diaphanous material of her draped gown. She had dark hair coiled modishly around her head and provocative eyes set in a flawless oval face.

Karen threw down the paper and got up. "I've got to go get my car," she said irritably, and stomped up the stairs to dress.

She couldn't picture Lee booting that girl in the picture out of his Blazer as unceremoniously as he had her yesterday afternoon. In fact, she couldn't imagine the girl in the paper *in* his Blazer. He probably had a Ferrari or a Porsche for her benefit.

Angrily, she yanked on a pair of jeans and a pink tube top with spaghetti straps, dragged a comb through her hair and anchored it with a clasp at the back of her neck. She felt angry because she had no business feeling angry or jealous, when all she wanted was that damned interview!

To Karen's surprise, the blue Blazer was parked in front of her house when she drove home in her little yellow VW. Her heart bumped against her ribs, and she had to remind herself that she was angry and she wasn't going to cooperate in his little game, whatever that was. She sat in the car, her fists pounding the steering wheel, until the sun beating on the metal roof drove her into the house.

The sound of voices led her to the kitchen. Lee lounged in one chair, his legs crossed on another, the pointed toes of his boots aiming at the ceiling, his hat on the table. Elsie sat across from him, her eyes bright and interested under her fluffy silver hair. Both of them looked at Karen as if she had interrupted something important.

"What are you doing here, Payne?" Karen demanded.

"Karen Jane!" Elsie reprimanded sharply.

Lee grinned cheerfully. "I just came to see your mother. She's nicer than you. Sit down." He pushed a plate of pastries toward her. "I brought some Danish. If you're good, you can have one."

She couldn't hang onto her anger; it melted away in the presence of his obvious pleasure at seeing her. Pulling out a chair, she sat down and took a roll. "I don't like bringing my work home with me," she said around a bite.

"You didn't bring me. I followed."

"That's worse."

"I don't have to be work, you know. If you relax and enjoy yourself, you're more likely to get what you want, catch me at a vulnerable moment, if you know what I mean." He picked up his hat and settled it rakishly over his eyebrows, then reached out to brush at the front of her shirt. "Crumbs," he said. "You're a messy eater, Hunter."

Karen slapped his hand away and glanced at Elsie. She was resting her chin on her hands, smiling.

Lee looked her over. "As long as you've got your play clothes on, why don't we take a ride?" His costume hadn't changed, except that he was wearing a clean white shirt.

"I suppose you've already asked my mother if I could come out and play," Karen said, finishing the last crumbs of the pastry.

"Yup, and she said, 'Get that girl out from under my feet—always in my way, that Karen Jane.'" His teeth were white against his tan when he smiled. "'She never goes out and has any fun, so why don't you take her in hand?' That's what she said."

Elsie got up. "Thanks a lot. I said no such thing, so don't glower at me, Karen Jane. I'm going downstairs, and you two can argue on your own." She left.

Karen took another Danish and munched.

"Well?" Lee asked.

"Well, what?"

"Want to go visit my sister?" He lifted his feet off the chair and leaned forward to rest his elbows on the table and play with his coffee cup.

"Your sister?" Karen always seemed to be six or seven steps behind what he had in mind.

He glanced up. "If you're still interested in knowing all about me, you might as well start with the basics."

She stared at him and put the roll on the plate. "Are you saying that you have decided to let me write about you?"

His black eyes pierced her briefly. "As long as you let it happen my way. And"—he reached out to press one forefinger against her short, straight nose—"as long as I get to approve every single word you write. I can still sue if you don't oblige me, and don't you forget it."

Her eyes glistened with anticipation. She wrapped her hand around his threatening finger. "I know, I know, sue my pretty little pants off." She laughed and gave his finger back to him. "Why did you decide to let me do it?"

"I developed the pictures we took of you. I like them. They don't lie."

She didn't understand but decided not to push for an explanation. "I'd better change into something more suitable if we're going to see your sister." Karen wondered what she would be like— probably out of the same mold as the girl in the paper, or the receptionist, for that matter.

"You're fine. Are those good hiking shoes? I want to show you something afterwards."

She frowned slightly. "Hiking?"

He misinterpreted her frown. "Well chaperoned, I promise."

She laughed—a chaperone was just as well—and held up a foot in a blue-and-white tennis shoe. "These are the best I can come up with."

"Let's go, then," he said, and led the way to the Blazer.

Lee's sister lived in Arvada, a suburb northwest of Denver, on a hill where the houses overlooked the entire city and a good portion of the mountain range, from the far distant Pike's Peak to Mount Evens, barely showing its hump over its less majestic brothers. Karen caught her breath at the view.

The house was large and multi-leveled, but with an aura of disrepair that made it look like a weed in the neat flower bed of well-kept homes in the neighborhood. Lee stopped his truck in front of it and sat with his hands on the wheel for a moment. Finally, he turned to Karen and said, "Nita doesn't care much for women. She might give you a hard time. Think you can take it?"

Karen looked back questioningly. "I've got a thick skin, Payne." That wasn't entirely true, but her curiosity was tumbling pell-mell by now, and forewarned was forearmed, so she imagined she could take anything that was dished out. Whatever that might be.

"Glad to hear that, Hunter," Lee said, and smiled, brushing her cheek with his knuckles. "I could have sworn you had pale, thin skin."

They picked their way up the walk, through a minefield of toys. Lee opened the front door without ringing, and they went in.

A stereo blasted country-western music from two large speakers on either side of the playroom. A television set competed loudly, with Bugs Bunny cartoons. Two little girls deserted the TV set, screaming shrilly as they leaped on Lee, clinging to his legs and arms as if with tentacles, squealing, "Uncle Pee Lee."

Karen watched with an open mouth as he allowed them to wrestle him to the carpet, where they pinned him down and rifled his pockets for candy, then deserted him to finger their prizes and squabble over who got to wear his hat.

Lee got up on his hands and knees to switch off the television set and turn down the stereo. "Hi, Kenny," he said to the man watching tolerantly in an easy chair. A beer can was lifted in return greeting.

Lee sat down cross-legged in the middle of the

floor, as his sister came out of the kitchen. He waved a hand toward her. "And that, Karen, is my one and only sister. The *only* family I have, for that matter. Nita, this is Karen, a friend of mine." His eyes were on Karen, checking her reaction.

Nita wore tight white shorts and a blue blouse that stretched and gaped around the generosity of her bosom. The rest of her was as slim and svelte as a Barbie doll. A mop of unbelievably pale blond hair cascaded down her shoulders. Her light-blue eyes had as much expression as a doll's.

After a greeting to Karen, Nita dropped on the floor beside Lee and put her arm around him, her face tender with possessive warmth. "Why didn't you warn us you were coming, Pee Lee? I'd have cleaned the house. It's a mess."

With a quick glance, Karen agreed. A visible film of dust covered everything, except where the wet bottoms of glasses had left their marks on the tabletops. Every ashtray overflowed.

Nita's husband, Kenny, got up from his chair to stand in front of Karen and grin admiringly. He was big and heavily muscled, with no shirt covering the thick brown hair on his chest. His enormous hand swallowed Karen's, and he didn't let go. "So you're Lee's new girl, are you?" He looked her up and down.

"Not exactly," Karen said, forcibly retrieving her hand.

Kenny laughed, a deep rumble. "I can't say you're much like the ones we're used to, but I trust his taste; he knows where it's at." He held up the can he was holding. "Want a beer?"

"No. No, thank you," Karen answered, and retreated to sit in a chair across the room. It strained her imagination to think of these people as the great P. Lee Payne's family. He might be a little eccentric in his dressing habits, but he obviously had class.

The two little girls drew close after Karen sat down; they were curious and friendly as puppies. Ann and Penny, eight and six, answered her questions shyly, then responded eagerly to Karen's gentle teasing. She looked at Nita, wondering what kind of a mother she was, then at Lee, completely bewildered. He had been watching her talk to the girls.

He reached over to tweak one child's bare ankle. "Hey, if you kids get cleaned up, we'll take you for a ride." They leaped off the arm of Karen's chair and raced for the stairs with birdlike screeches.

Lee got off the floor and settled himself on the arm of Karen's chair, his arm resting behind her along the back. "I guess I should have asked you first, Nita. Can we take the girls up to my place? Chaperones, you know," he said, smirking at Karen.

Nita nodded and lit a cigarette to blow smoke at the ceiling in a huff.

Kenny took a drink from his can and wiped the foam off his lip with the back of his hand. "What you want a chaperone for, man?" he asked, leering at Karen.

Nita laughed, a tinkling sound. She looked at Karen. "Because he's picked up with the last living virgin over the age of thirteen, that's why." She laughed again and arched her back to give the blouse a dangerous stretch. "I didn't think there was such a thing anymore. I'll bet I'm right, huh, Karen?"

"That's enough, Nita," Lee said. His voice didn't leave room for argument, and Nita dropped her head, grinning, as Lee started a neutral conversation with Kenny about the construction project he worked on, much to Karen's relief. Her face burned.

The girls came bounding downstairs with polished faces and clean shorts, their taffy-colored hair slicked back. The four of them left the house, climbed in the Blazer and headed for the mountains.

Karen sat close to the car door, still smarting from Nita's taunt. After they were well underway, Lee laughed and said, "I warned you."

"You don't have to say I told you so," Karen snapped.

After a few miles of silence, he asked, "Well, are you?"

"Am I what?" She glanced back to where the little girls were listening alertly.

"What she said."

"Payne, you *are* a pain, and I don't see how it could possibly be any of your business." Karen folded her arms angrily and glared out the side window.

Penny leaned over the back of the seat, her eyes big and worried. "Don't you like Uncle Pee Lee, Karen?"

Karen turned to smile at the child. "I love him. He's a doll."

Penny's face lit up with a smile, missing the sarcasm. "Oh, I do too." She threw her arms around his neck in a stranglehold.

"Hey, watch it." He laughed, loosening her arms with one hand and keeping a careful eye on the road. "I don't know if I can stand all this affection in one day." He grinned at Karen. She stuck out her tongue at him and turned to the window to watch the hills close in.

By the time they reached Lee's house in the mountains, Karen's ruffled feelings had smoothed out. The little girls wouldn't let her pout, and they drew her out with a hunger for attention that she couldn't ignore. Besides, the enormous, cobalt-blue sky, with its fluffy, floating clouds, and the heady scent of pine and smog-free air didn't nurture anger.

The girls tumbled out of the Blazer and ran like chipmunks around the yard. They greeted every bush and tree as an old friend.

Lee unlocked the door and stood aside for Karen to enter.

"Oh, no," she said, shaking her head. "You go first."

"Chicken," he said, laughing, and led her in. The dogs met him with waving tails. They were just as big as Karen remembered, but after an initial rumble of warning, they checked her over and tolerated her presence. She followed Lee to the kitchen.

The kitchen was sparkling clean, as was the rest of the house. "Do you do your own housework?" Karen asked. "This place is so clean it's painful."

"I like things organized," Lee said, packing sandwiches and fruit in a backpack. "A woman comes in to do the tedious stuff, but mostly it takes care of itself. I planned it that way."

Nervously, Karen edged closer to him, eyeing the German Shepherd beside her. "Lee, this dog is biting me," she said tightly. The animal ran its teeth over Karen's thigh with little nipping clicks at the denim of her pants, not quite pinching, but too close for comfort.

"She's not biting you, she's tasting you. I think she likes you."

"For lunch?" she quavered, pressing herself against his side, afraid if she pushed the dog away it would attack her in earnest.

He laughed. "Freak, go lay down," he said, and to Karen's relief, Freak obeyed. "Don't worry about her," he said, "she's a pussycat."

Still glued to Lee's side, she watched the dog, which had its eyes on her leg, its tongue hanging out hopefully. "A pussycat," Karen said; "she looks like a killer to me."

The girls tumbled into the kitchen. Karen gasped as both dogs leaped to attention, ready to rip the tiny bodies with their fangs. All four met in a giggling tangle of flailing feet and waving paws on the floor, with happy shouts and delighted whines.

Lee laughed. "Right! Killers. Both of them." He swung the backpack over his shoulders. "Everybody out," he called over the commotion. The dogs and girls raced through the back door.

Karen followed them out. "Where do you think you're taking me?" she asked.

"I thought you'd like to climb a mountain," Lee said, nudging her across the rough grass. "It's not much of a mountain, really, technically speaking, but it's the best I have to offer at short notice."

Karen looked dubiously at the path that wound up the hill behind the house at a sixty-degree angle. It was pocked with rocks and boulders, bushes and gravel slides. The girls had scrambled halfway up, chasing the dogs, which kicked dust and gravel in their faces with scrabbling claws. "I can't climb up there," she said firmly. "You're out of your mind."

"Why not? If you can put one foot in front of the other, you can climb it."

Karen leaned her head way back to look at the top of the mountain. She shook away a feeling of vertigo.

"Want me to carry you?" Lee asked, and made a motion to follow through on his offer.

"You stay away from me, Payne," Karen said. She took the first step up the path and found herself committed.

Scrabbling for handholds, slipping and stumbling, she plowed her way up, with Lee right behind her. Brush scratched her face, and her knuckles bled from grazing against the granite boulders. Once she slipped and lost her hold, tobogganing a few yards down on her stomach. Lee caught her in his arms and set her on her feet, pushing her on her way. She set her teeth grimly and went on.

The climb seemed to take forever before Karen grabbed at a tree trunk at the top rim of the hill. She clutched the tree and dragged her trembling legs over the edge. Heaving and blowing, she flopped on her back on the patchy grass. Both of the dogs pushed forward to lick her face. If this was what it took to be accepted by them, she thought, covering her face with both arms, she wasn't certain it was worth it.

Lee pushed the dogs away and sat down beside her. "What do you think of it?" he asked, looking away into the distance.

Karen looked at him through the black dots bouncing in front of her eyes. He was in his element on this hill, relaxed and open, and so very wonderful to look at.

Pulling herself up to a sitting position, she followed his gaze.

The gray-green, hazy mountains rolled away to meet the sky on the horizon, dark evergreens spilling down their sides, punctuated with the lighter, warm green of aspens and smudged with red and orange brush, a hint of the coming fall. The air had the heady scent of vintage champagne, and was as intoxicating. The sound of a hidden stream in the distance, rushing down a grade over rocks and logs, almost tempted Karen to get up on her tortured legs to run and find it. She looked at Lee, smiling with awe.

He had pushed his hat to the back of his head, watching her, as if he could see the view in the delight on her face. Their smiles met in understanding and pleasure. Lee's arm crept around her, his hand warm and insistent on her rib cage, pulling her tentatively closer, a questioning, inviting look in his eyes. The touch of his long, hard thigh on her leg kindled responses she had been trying so very hard to control.

She glanced at his lips and knew they were coming closer, then felt her face tilting up and her own mouth parting to meet his.

The spell was shattered when a piping voice announced, "I'm hungry." They pulled apart as Ann plopped her small body beside them. "Are you going to sit here all day?"

"Chaperones," Lee muttered and lay back to stare at the sky. "I'd liked to have sat like that all day," he answered.

"But I'm hungry. Make him get up, Karen."

"I can't do a thing with him." Karen laughed and got up to look down the trail she had climbed.

From the top, it looked straight down. "My Lord," she exclaimed, "I'll never make it back down again."

Lee got up to stand beside her. "Then we'd better eat. You'll have to stoke up if you're going to spend the rest of your life up here. Starvation isn't the prettiest way to go, so they say. Come on."

He took her hand and led her to a small lean-to set against a couple of stunted trees. It was sturdy, with the wide side mostly in glass. Unlocking the door, he brought out a blanket to spread on the ground and unpacked his back pack.

They sat side by side on the blanket, the dogs beside them, watching every bite, while the girls scampered over the hillside, eating on the run. A breeze drifted around them, carrying the scent of hot leaves, late summer, and distant glaciers.

It was pleasant, too pleasant, Karen thought. She could easily become addicted to the intoxicating clear air. And to the man sprawled beside her. It was folly to delude herself that he was meant for her. She sighed and reminded herself she was here with him for information and nothing else.

"Why the deep sigh?" Lee asked, his eyes warm on her face. His hand covered hers, then slid slowly up her arm and to her shoulder. Every hair on her arms seemed to rise, and when he leaned forward, his lips aiming for hers, her heart leaped. When his mouth touched hers, heat spread through her body.

The hand on her shoulder continued its slow, tantalizing quest until it rested on her breast. She gasped at the explosion of sensation and drew away reluctantly. "Don't, Lee," she whispered. "The girls . . ."

Only the sound of their childish voices broke

the silence that fell when he pulled away from her. Wrapping her arms around her knees, she looked at him. "Why did you take me to meet your sister, Lee?"

He looked back at her from under the brim of his hat. "If you're going to write about me intelligently, then you have to know who I am and where I'm coming from, don't you?" He laid his hat on the ground beside him.

Karen watched the sun glint blue in his dark hair. Her fingers itched to touch it, run through it. "Why haven't you married, Lee? You seem to enjoy children and that kind of thing."

He turned toward her, and his black eyes hit hers over the white of his grin. "Because I hadn't met you," he said.

"Oh, sure," she said, and wrinkled her nose at him. He got up and began to gather the remains of lunch. Karen followed him into the small building, then stared around in amazement. It was a studio with several oil paintings in different stages of creation, some leaning against the walls, a couple on easels. The smell of paint and turpentine stung her nose. The paintings were done with the same technique as the picture of the children that had troubled her in his living room. All the colors were harsh and demanding, a riot of confusion, until she moved to search for the scene portrayed. They were fascinating and compelling.

"You're a surprising man, Payne," she said. "Even to my uneducated eye, this isn't amateurish stuff. I didn't know you painted."

"You don't do your research very thoroughly, do you, Hunter?" he said, tossing bread crusts and plastic wrap in a trash can. "We can't have that if you're going to be a famous reporter someday."

He was right, and it irritated her to have it pointed out. She touched the rough surface of one of the finished canvases and followed the letters of his signature. "What does the 'P' stand for in P. Lee Payne?"

"Passionate," he answered, standing just behind her. His breath tickled her ear.

"Get away from me, Payne." She laughed.

"In that case, it stands for poor. Poor Lee Payne."

"You're nuts. 'P' is for psycho." She walked away from him to look at another picture. If she had stayed close to him, she would have been in his arms. She wasn't the type of girl who could sleep with a man and enjoy him without falling for him head over heels, and she didn't care to drag herself out of another disappointing love affair.

The picture she was studying was a mountain scene. She stepped close and watched the form disappear into flecks and daubs of color. "It's so confusing," she said. "How can you tell what you're doing, with no outlines and no orientation?"

"I have a picture in my mind, and my hands have the practical training—they know what has to be done to create form and effect. The warm colors come out at you, to give an illusion of configuration. The paintings come from my subconscious. What you see is a reflection of my psyche." He smiled wryly. "Do they make you feel comfortable?" She shook her head. "Then beware, Karen Jane."

She walked around the room slowly. Each painting had at least one, sometimes several, lonely, isolated figures in it. She looked at him speculatively. Did it express loneliness? But a man like Lee, handsome, popular, wealthy, couldn't be lonely.

Lee had his foot on a chair, leaning on his knee, watching her. "What about the children in the painting in the living room; are they taken from your subconscious?" she asked.

"Come sit in the sun," he said. "I'll tell you a fairy tale."

They sat on the blanket. Karen propped herself up on her elbows, and Lee lay back with his hands under his head. "Once upon a time," he started in his deep, pleasant voice, "there were two children who never did much of anything fun. One day their mother took them to a lake. Sloan's Lake." He cocked an eye at Karen. "Ever been there?" She nodded, and he went on. "It was a day like today, hot and sunny. That was back when the lake was a real lake, with beaches and no pollution. The kids bought hot dogs and ice cream cones and splashed in the water. They were free—no grown-ups, just pure pleasure."

Karen studied his face curiously. There was a pained line between his dark brows. He felt her watching him and pushed his hat over his nose. Then he went on, personalizing the story. "Nita was ten and I was six. I couldn't have drowned if I had tried. Nita dragged me around like a rag doll, a mother duck with her duckling." He paused with a little smile on his lips, remembering.

Karen looked at him, frowning. He had to be at least thirty-four. That would put Nita in the neighborhood of thirty-eight. It was hard to believe that doll-like woman with the blond hair was approaching middle age. "She must have been a pretty little girl," she said.

Lee laughed. "She was the saddest-looking kid you've ever seen, skinny and pale, with hair like limp spaghetti. She had a perpetual cold, maybe allergies, complete with red eyes and a runny nose. Later on, she learned to elaborate on the good points she did have, but unfortunately, she overdoes it a little." He sighed.

"But to get on with the story, the day progressed into afternoon, then evening. The sun went down, and it started to get cold. The wind came up, and the money was gone, so we couldn't buy anything to eat. I started crying. I've been reminded that I did a lot of that."

Karen turned on her stomach to prop her chin on her hands and watch Lee as he talked.

"It seems our mother had forgotten where she left us," he went on. "She had been enjoying her free day by drinking a little. The stars came out; it was as cold as hell. Nita thought she knew the way home, so we started walking. It was seven miles and it took us two hours, with me whining and dragging my feet, all the way. Nita didn't shed a tear; she just held my hand and brought me home." He shifted his body, reaching under his back to pull out a stone that he threw down the hill.

"What happened when you got home?" Karen asked. His mother must have been frantic. What kind of a mother had she been, anyway?

"Seems our mother had remembered, finally, where she was supposed to pick us up, but of course we weren't at the lake when she got there. We were sitting on the front steps when she got home." He pushed his hat back and glanced at Karen. "And that, Karen Jane, is one of my happier childhood memories. I keep the picture in my living room so I'll be able to remember the lake and the hot dogs."

Karen sat up. She looked at Lee, then at the

clouds drifting across the sky and at the muted mountains in the distance. She couldn't think of a response. She felt like crying . . . sobbing, really.

Lee stood up, towering over her. "You're getting pink, Hunter. We'd better go."

"Pink?" she repeated stupidly.

"Pink. Too much sun isn't good, even for girls with skin as thick as you think yours is." He whistled shrilly through his teeth, bringing the girls and dogs at a run.

Karen found it difficult to pull herself out of the story he had told. It shocked and grieved her. She watched him put away the blanket and lock the small house. She wondered how he had become what he was, if that was how his early life had been.

When she moved to follow him to the path down the hill, her skin puckered on her shoulders, screaming out against the skimpy straps of her sun top. Her skin wasn't a fraction as thick as she might have wished.

The trek down the hill wasn't as difficult as she had anticipated. The four of them simply sat down and slid down the steep incline as if it were a sledding run. The girls tumbled on ahead, with the dogs barking alongside, and Karen slid down more cautiously, with Lee right behind her. She couldn't help laughing, enjoying the foolishness of it, bumping off boulders and losing her balance, with Lee's warm hands always ready to right her.

She could barely stand on her feet at the bottom. Lee laughed and brushed leaves and dust off her. "Hunter, you are a mess," he said.

Inspecting herself, she had to agree. Her jeans were torn; her hands were scratched and black with dirt. "Payne, I don't know how I let you talk me into something so crazy." She grimaced as she pulled a twig out of a snarl in her hair. "I loved it, though. I've never been on a mountain like this before. But I was supposed to be asking you questions, taking down information. I didn't even remember."

He gave her a long, piercing look. "I thought you told me you were very smart. I've given you half your article"—he took her chin—"if you've got enough marbles in this dense head of yours to sort it out and put it down in a way that I can accept."

Then he dropped a kiss on her forehead, withdrew his hand and smiled. "You're one of the few people who has been on that particular mountain with me."

He left her to mull over that statement. She touched her chin, where the print of his fingers was etched indelibly.

The drive back was sleepy and quiet. Lee had withdrawn into himself and Karen couldn't bring him out. He dropped the girls off, then Karen. His good-bye was so abrupt that it seemed he could hardly wait for her to get out of the Blazer so he could speed away.

Five

Even after having spent all day Sunday immobile in bed, rubbing cream on the sunburn on her face and shoulders and arms, Karen's body still protested in agony as she struggled through her work on Monday.

At least the heat wave had broken in the late afternoon. A cool breeze drifted in through her office window as she finished the last odds and ends of paper work before she could go home.

When her desk was clear, Karen looked in the mirror back of her door. When she lifted her arms to run a comb through her hair, the skin on her shoulders stretched like tissue.

As she reached out to open the door, it burst open, startling a yelp out of her.

Nita, Lee's sister, breezed in, wafting a cloud of musky perfume ahead of her, crisp and impeccable in a pair of white pants that were molded to her hips. "Hi," she said in her breathy little voice. "They told me up front that you would be back here and that I could come find you."

Karen stood speechless. Nita was the last person she would have expected to come find her. Still smarting from the "last living virgin" dig, she was in no mood for a sparring match today, of all days. She smiled stiffly.

Nita looked at Karen's face. "Wow," she said, and laughed her tinkling little laugh. "Pee Lee really got to you, didn't he? If you're done here, I'll buy you a nice cold drink with lots of ice to help put out the fire." When Karen started to shake her head, Nita pleaded, "Please, I've got to talk to you."

Karen gritted her teeth and gave in, out of curiosity. What could Nita possibly want from her? "Sure, why not?"

The bar was named The Mile High Hi, unbelievably, and soft rock music accompanied them to a booth. Karen suspected she looked fluorescent under a spotlight that beamed a bright glow on them.

A barmaid with a ruffled skirt took their order, a scotch on the rocks for Nita and a white wine for Karen.

After a sip, Nita played with the glass, connecting wet rings into a chain on the table, her lower lip turned out in a pout. Finally, she said, "I want to apologize to you. I wasn't very nice when you were at the house Saturday." She looked up at Karen with her China-blue doll's eyes. "I don't know why I say things like that. I open my mouth and I never know what's going to come out."

Karen wasn't ready to accept an apology. "As you can see, I survived," she said noncommittally.

Nita's eyes begged. She touched Karen's hand

with fingers icy cold from the glass. "Please, please forgive me. I can't take the words back into my mouth. If I could, I would. Don't be mad at me."

It was impossible to hold a grudge against the doll-eyed, baby-voiced woman. Karen smiled. "Okay, I forgive you. It's forgotten." She laughed slightly. Nita was at least twelve years older than she, but she made Karen feel like a mean mother.

Nita sighed deeply and sat back. "Oh, I do appreciate it." She sipped her scotch. "Will you do me a favor? Tell Pee Lee I've been nice. Please?"

Karen raised her eyebrows. So Lee had brought on this fit of remorse. She leaned forward, with her elbows on the table. "I can't believe it bothered him that much. He thought it was funny and laughed about it later."

Nita bit at her fingertip, looking at Karen. "He's always laughing; that doesn't mean he thinks it's funny." She leaned forward. "You will tell him, won't you? That I've been nice?"

"If I see him again, I'll tell him."

Nita laughed. "Oh, you'll see him again." She sobered. "Just don't hurt him. He's my baby, and I don't want him hurt."

"He's kind of a big baby, isn't he? And how could I hurt him? Me of all people."

"You especially." Finely plucked eyebrows lowered over Nita's eyes. "What do you want from him?"

"I want to write an article about him."

She waved a hand irritably. "Besides that?"

"Nothing," Karen said, half embarrassed. "I hardly know the man."

"See? That's what I mean." Nita waved to the barmaid for another scotch. "All his other women want something from him—his money, his reputation, his body. He knows how to handle that; he expects it. *Are* you a virgin?"

"I don't know what difference that makes, whether I am or not," Karen answered, visibly annoyed.

"See, that's what I'm talking about." A slim finger jabbed the air. "You're the virgin *type*, and Lee's going to get hurt. You'll never accept him the way he is."

What way was he? Karen wondered. "Look," she assured Nita, "I'm not looking for a relationship. But why do you feel you have to protect him? He's a grown man."

"I've always had to protect Lee." She lit a cigarette and smoked it like a sparrow pecking seed, in quick little puffs. "I took care of Lee when he was little. Our mother had to work, and she didn't have much time for us."

She smiled tenderly. "He was such a cute little baby. The first time he cuddled his head into my shoulder, ∴ made him mine."

She shook her head and frowned. "She couldn't seem to get over my father's dying, and comforted herself with drinking. Then, when she was drunk, she'd yell, usually at Lee. Philip Lee! Always Philip Lee! That's why he doesn't use Philip anymore; he can't stand the sound of it.

"Mother's dead now," she added, frowning unhappily. "She died when Lee was only fifteen."

"What about your father?" Karen asked. "What was he like?"

"He was a musician—he played the trumpet." Nita took a deep swallow from her glass. "We had some bad times, with never enough money, even though Mother worked as a waitress. She never got over losing my father, and it was hard for her to bring two children up alone."

Her eyes seemed lost in the past, her brow puckered. "We got by somehow, though."

She finished the scotch in her glass and stared intently at the ice cubes. "After Mother died, Lee went to a foster home—Luther and Marty Tillson's. They seemed to be good to him."

Karen tucked that bit of information away in her head. Her more immediate concern was to get Nita out of the bar before she had another drink.

Fresh air seemed to revive her, and she drove Karen back to the parking lot behind the *Review*.

Karen watched her drive away, wondering what it must have been like to grow up with the kind of responsibilities Nita had assumed. She must have had no childhood. It explained a great deal about the adult Nita.

As she walked to her car and drove home, she smiled wryly at the thought that she might be dangerous to P. Lee Payne. It seemed to be the other way around.

After Karen's encounter with Nita, the rest of the week progressed calmly. With September's issue of the magazine printed and out, the staff relaxed to banter and gossip, unlimbering themselves before the next deadline.

Karen hadn't seen Lee since Saturday, and her mood fluctuated between relief that she didn't have to deal with the disturbing sensations he initiated in her, and disappointment that she couldn't finish the sketch she had started. She had hoped to have the article on him in the October issue of the *Review*.

When she walked into her office on Friday morning, a couple of brown-socked crossed feet greeted her from her desk.

Closing the door softly, Karen walked in and shook her head. Lee had managed to arrange his substantial frame in her swivel chair, tipped back to give an appearance of luxurious comfort. His fingers were laced across his stomach and his head had fallen back, the mouth slightly open to breathe soft snores.

He had obviously been out the night before. He was dressed in a pair of pale-tan western-cut trousers and a sport jacket of light-brown leather so smooth and soft that Karen's fingers itched to touch it.

His hat lay on the desk beside his feet. She picked it up and sat in its place to look at him. With a night's growth of dark beard accentuating the small scar on his chin, he should have looked dissipated, but he didn't. He simply looked vulnerable . . . and very sexy. She sniffed at a faint scent of expensive women's perfume about him and smiled. It didn't take a detective to know what he had been doing last night. She looked pensively at the thick black lashes resting on his tanned cheeks, at the curve of his lips, soft in sleep, and sighed, then shrugged irritably.

Shaking his toes, she said, "Rise and shine, Payne."

He woke with a blank, disoriented glare. Then he recognized her and relaxed to rub at his face blearily, sandpapering the stubble on his jaw and running his fingers through the dark hair that lay mussed and wavy on his forehead.

"Do you always look this bad when you wake up

in the morning?" she asked. "What are you doing in my office, if I may ask?"

Lee uncrossed his legs and lifted them to the floor with an effort, grimacing. "My feet are asleep," he complained.

"I'm not surprised," she said, and watched him fold his arms on the desk to drop his head on them.

"I'm not running a flophouse here, you know. How'd you get in?"

He lifted his head to prop his chin on a fist. "I picked the lock."

She laughed. "Of course—silly me, what a dumb question. Why?"

"I was tired. I didn't want to drive home."

"Why didn't you stay over with her?"

"Who?"

"Whoever wears that perfume you reek of."

He put his nose to the leather sleeve of his jacket. "Oh, her." Then he gave Karen an impish look. "Jealous?"

"Not likely," she said quickly.

He reached out and put an arm around her waist. "Then give me a good morning kiss. Maybe I'll turn into a frog."

Karen got down off the desk and away from his arm. "It'd be a waste of time; no one would notice if you did."

"I look that bad, do I?" He rubbed his chin again. Then he looked at his watch. "Nine o'clock! I've got to go into Denver this morning. Damn, I don't want to drive way up to Evergreen and back." He reached down to pull on a pair of richly embroidered cowboy boots.

Karen still held his hat, turning it, running her fingers around the edge. It was a new one, of crisp beige felt. She tried to imagine what it might be like to wake up beside Lee each morning, to kiss him awake. The picture in her mind was entrancing! She put the hat down on the desk and frowned. She had no intention of joining this cowboy's stable of mares. If only she could finish the article and be done with him.

Reaching in her purse, she took out her keys and jingled them. "If you want to, you can clean up at my house. My mother's out, but I'm sure you can find everything. There's a new toothbrush in the drawer in the bathroom, and if you don't mind using a razor that's touched legs, mine is in the medicine cabinet."

He lifted his head and grinned. "That's an interesting thought, Hunter. Thanks." He reached out for the keys, his fingers lingering on hers. She pulled her own back as if she'd been burned.

"And," Karen said, "if you have time, later in the day, maybe you could come back and I can get the rest of what I need for the article about you. I'd like to finish it."

He frowned and got up to walk to the door. "I don't feel like that kind of hassle today." Then his face brightened as he reached for the doorknob. "And yes, I always look this bad when I wake up in the morning. Why did you want to know?" he asked, grinning.

"Get out, Payne," she said, laughing self-consciously. "I've got work to do."

But she didn't have enough to do to keep her thoughts channeled away from the image of Lee waking up in the morning, in a big soft bed, stretching and reaching out . . .

"Hey, what are you daydreaming about?" Hank Mitchell stood in front of her desk with a sheaf of papers in his hand, grinning, dimples flashing in each cheek.

"Nothing special," Karen said quickly, her blush denying her words. "What can I do for you?"

"Lots, if you only would," Hank said pleasantly, and sat on the edge of the desk.

"Did you want me to look at this?" She took the papers out of his hand.

They spent the next hour and a half rewriting Hank's article and talking about the entertainment world, what they liked about plays and stage shows. It was pleasant, and the time passed quickly.

"Why don't you have dinner with me tonight?" Hank asked finally. "I know a place where I'll bet you haven't been. They have the most fantastic jazz band. It's dark and there's a lot of privacy."

Karen watched his cheek dimple. But . . . She opened her mouth to refuse. The jingle of keys interrupted her.

Lee stood in the doorway, clean and shaved, with his hat wedged down over his eyes, the key ring encircling the finger he held up. He walked across the room to place the keys intimately in Karen's palm. But if his fingers were soft on Karen's hand, his eyes were as hard as agate on Hank Mitchell.

He looked at Karen and gave her a beguiling smile. "An hour in your bed was magnificent. I'll take advantage of it again. Soon, I hope."

Karen glanced at the surprised look on Hank's face, then she glared at Lee and opened her mouth to protest.

He cut her off by nodding at the paperweight in Hank's hands. "You'd better keep your hands off that. It's valuable." Then he disappeared through the door without a backward glance.

Hank stared after him, then questioningly at Karen. "Would I be correct in assuming that I've been warned off by the urban cowboy? Why didn't you tell me you were involved with someone else?"

Karen shook her head and laughed weakly. "I'm not even going to try to explain that. But it wasn't . . . isn't what it appears to be. And, if that offer is still good, I'd love to go out with you tonight." Suddenly it seemed vital to have something besides Lee Payne happening in her life.

"Great," Hank said, smiling. "And I wish I could thank your friend. I didn't think you were going to go with me, before he came in." He stood up and handed the paperweight to her. "About seven-ish, then?"

Karen put the paperweight down and nodded.

Six

Saturday morning began luxuriously. Karen lay in her bed, lazily watching the sunlight filter through the drawn curtains. The night out with Hank Mitchell had been fun, and she thought about letting a relationship develop between them.

Stretching like a cat, she put away her thoughts and supposed if she had to think about letting a relationship form, it didn't have much going for it. Kicking the sheet off, she pulled herself up to sit cross-legged on the bed, yawning hugely. Then she smiled. It seemed she spent more time worrying about *not* letting a relationship develop between Lee and herself. The frustrating part of it was that he hadn't made an overture that could be repulsed. It was her own rebellious body playing with the idea. If only she could get that tantalizing article written, she could forget him. Yawning again, she scratched her knee and inspected the tan of her hand against the pale white of her leg and frowned. Who was she trying to fool? Lee Payne would be almost impossible to forget.

She decided her project for this weekend would be to tan the rest of her body. September had begun on Wednesday, and she knew its sun didn't have the impact of a good high-summer sun, but just lying outdoors with nothing to think about would be pleasant.

Pawing through her drawers, she unearthed an old pair of gym shorts, faded royal blue and frayed around the edges, and the skimpy top of a white bathing suit. When she had them on, she took a couple of oversized beach towels and went downstairs.

"Now what?" Elsie asked, peering at Karen over the paper.

Karen had a long strip of masking tape and was centering it on the edge of one towel. She taped the towel carefully along the line of her tan. "I'm going to lie in the sun, and I don't want to get a deeper tan on top until the rest catches up. I look like a butterscotch sundae."

Elsie shook her head and went back to the paper.

Karen spread the other towel on the grass in the backyard and carefully lay down without dislodging the towel taped to her chest. She pulled the towel over her arms and head and sighed contentedly. The eleven o'clock sun felt soothing, melting her muscles. She let her mind drift, dozing.

Until the ants found her. At least she supposed it was an ant marching across her stomach, tickling and aggravating her. "Damn," she muttered, extracting an arm from under her towel to brush it away.

It didn't take the hint. As soon as she had

gotten her arm back under the towel, it was back. Annoyed, Karen lifted the towel, then dropped it quickly back over her face. Lee sat on his heels beside her, running a blade of grass over the skin above her shorts. "What are you doing here, Payne?" she demanded through the towel.

"Actually, I'm wondering what the devil you're doing with a towel taped to your chest, Hunter." He laughed.

"It should be fairly obvious that I am relaxing in the privacy, please note, the privacy, of my own backyard, getting a tan." She lifted the towel to glare at him. "You've got your nerve coming around here after that show you put on in my office. An hour in my bed! What were you trying to do to my reputation?"

He made a face and rubbed his hand over his mouth. "I was hoping you would have forgotten that. Anyway, I did use your bed. I slept on it for an hour. I used your alarm clock, too."

Karen made a rude noise and dropped the towel over her face.

"Did you go?" he asked.

"Go where?"

"Out to dinner with the dimpled darling, in intimacy, darkness and privacy."

"What possible business is that of yours?" she demanded through the towel. "What do you want, Payne?"

Lee lay down on his stomach beside her and lifted the towel to look in her face. "Nothing. I just came to see you."

"Be careful, you're pulling the tape," she snapped. "Look, the only reason we know each other is because I want to write about you. I don't have any inclination to get involved outside of that. Understand?"

He took off his hat and arranged the towel over his head, his face six inches above hers. "Uh-huh," he agreed pleasantly.

Karen had to force down a laugh. "I know you've got dozens of classier females panting after you. Why don't you go give them a thrill?"

"Because I like you. You're unique. I've never known anyone who tapes towels to her chest." He smirked down at her. "It's too late in the season to get a tan. Why don't you come up in the mountains, to my place, say, where the thin air might let a little ultraviolet through?"

"Didn't you hear what I said? I'm not interested." The words didn't come easily with his dark, inviting eyes inches from hers.

"Who said *I* was? I'm making an appointment for an interview. You can ask me your tiresome questions." He smiled guilelessly. "I won't make any passes; I'll be working. You can lie in the sun with your silly towel over your head and ask away."

That sounded too good to be true. She frowned thoughtfully. "All right. I've got to take advantage of opportunity when it knocks." She sat up and peeled off the tape. "I'll go change."

"Why change? You look cute in those shorts." He stood up and pulled her to her feet. "I'll tell you what—I've got a pair of shorts that are even more tattered than those. When we get to the house I'll put them on, and that'll really be funny."

True to his promise, Lee changed into a pair of ragged cut-off jeans, topped by his bare, furry chest, and put on a pair of worn Addidas. He didn't look funny, Karen noticed. She wandered around his living room while he puttered in the kitchen packing a picnic lunch. It was a comfortable, beautiful home, and she knew she could easily come to like it too much.

The dogs pattered along beside her, and every now and then, the one called Freak nibbled at her leg. Karen recognized that it wasn't a threat, but a bid for attention. "Why do you call this dog Freak?" Karen called toward the kitchen. "She doesn't look freakish."

Lee looked through the door. "Pet her," he said. Karen did, rubbing the velvety ears. Freak's eyes closed slowly in ecstasy as she melted into a limp heap on the carpet. "That's why," he said. "She freaks out over attention. Whoever owned her before must have neglected her, so she doesn't know how to handle love."

Karen glanced at him. He seemed more serious than the statement called for. She rubbed Freak's neck, and then Sally's, so the other dog wouldn't feel neglected.

"You ready to climb?" Lee asked after a moment.

"Ready as I'll ever be," she answered.

It pleased Karen that the steep trail seemed much easier this time, but she still had to catch her breath at the top, looking out over the distant mountains, shrouded in a bluish autumn haze.

"The aspens are beginning to turn," Lee said, pointing out the patches of golden lemon-yellow dotting the dusky green of the evergreens on the hillsides.

"So beautiful," Karen murmured, pulling in a huge breath of clean air scented with decaying warm leaves.

Seasonal change was exhilarating. Or was it the stimulating presence of the tanned, muscular man beside her? "I thought you were going to work," she said when she looked up to find him watching her.

Lee deliberately moved his arm to brush, ever so slowly, the bare skin of her shoulder. A tingle shot to her fingertips and to her toes. He laughed softly and walked away to push the glass doors of the studio wide open. He spread the blanket on the ground and said, "There you are, Hunter. Do you want to eat first, or worship the sun? Would you like me to tape your towel?"

"Never mind," she said, and sat down to hug her knees. "I'm not hungry yet, unless you are. I'd rather watch you do whatever it is you do."

He grinned and went into the studio to squeeze paint onto his palette. The painting on the easel was of a woman, a portrait, her face devoid of expression or personality. The entire picture was in shades of green.

"You said I could ask questions," Karen said inquiringly.

"Ask away," he answered. "But after you get done with your prying, I get to ask you some of my own, agreed?"

"I suppose that's fair enough," Karen said. She studied the picture. "Why is that woman green? Is she a martian?"

"The green is meant to gray the reds and pinks that I'm about to add, which'll give her life, I hope, when I'm finished." He stood back and contemplated the woman. "I'm doing this on commission." He mentioned a name Karen had read several times in the paper. "It's his wife. I don't generally like to work for anyone, but he's a friend of mine, so I agreed to do it. I find it restricting, creatively, to try to please someone else."

He spent some time daubing the canvas with a

palette knife and standing back to study the effect. "Don't you use brushes?" Karen asked.

"No. The knife gives a stronger, more vibrant texture." He glanced at her and smiled. "Besides, I hate to clean brushes, and all the knife takes is a swipe of a cloth."

He worked on the picture for several minutes, introducing deep reds around the curve of the face. "She's an interesting lady," he said. "I've spent quite a bit of time with her, getting to know her. I like her. I don't like to paint a sitting model. I'd rather know the person, her mannerisms, her reactions, her thoughts, and put my impressions on canvas. Anyone can reproduce a likeness. I'm interested in the essence. The camera can capture the essence to some degree, but not like a palette knife and paint and nosiness. That's why I've more or less given up photography; it's restricting." He glanced at her. "You got that down?"

"You didn't give me time to bring my paper and pencil."

"Remember it, then, bright girl." He pulled a chair up with the toe of one foot and sat down to stare at the painting. "This woman is Joe's second wife. He's crazy about her. And she thinks the world of him. Odd marriage." He scratched his chest pensively, leaving four trails of deep red paint in the curly black hair.

Karen laughed. "Isn't that the way it's supposed to be?"

Lee glanced at her and grinned. "So the romance novels say."

Stretching out on her stomach, Karen rested her chin on her hands. "How much do you get for a painting like that? Or am I out of line in asking?"

"What do you think it's worth?"

"I haven't the faintest idea."

"Make a guess."

She lifted her head and watched him contemplate his work with narrowed eyes, trying to think of an outrageous amount. "Two thousand dollars?"

He rubbed his chin and left a streak of white. "Add a zero and you're in the ballpark." With a glance in her direction, he added, "But that's a special price for a friend, of course."

"Good lord, Payne, I'm impressed."

"Well, I'm glad something about me finally impresses you, Hunter."

Lots about him impressed her. The delicate play of his strong muscles under his smooth skin, the curve of his nose, those dark, dark eyes . . . but she didn't think he needed to know that. "Why did you photograph me last week?" she asked. "Am I going to see the pictures?"

"I couldn't believe you were the naive, gullible, innocent pest you seemed to be, so I checked it out. The camera doesn't lie if you know how to handle the subject." He rocked on the back legs of the chair, looking at his painting, smiling.

Karen squirmed, half embarrassed, and changed position. "Well, was I?"

He laughed. "Worse."

"I can't stand the suspense. When can I see them?"

He shrugged. "I don't know. I'm working on them."

Karen watched him carefully apply paint to the woman's face. When he sat back, she asked, "You don't let yourself trust, really trust, many people, do you?"

A look of black lightning hit her. "No. I spent the first half of my life being lonely. It wasn't your basic good experience. I don't care to leap in for more of the same."

"Then why am I here? I've told you as bluntly as I can that I'm not interested in a relationship."

"That's the difference." He laid the knife aside and stood up to lean back against the table beside him, his arms folded across his chest. "It's the one who promises everything, with the sky the limit, who worries me. They usually carry hell around in their hearts." He stared at her for a few seconds. "And you'd better never write anything like that about me in your little blurb."

"I wouldn't have, even if you hadn't told me," Karen said, a little hurt that he thought she might have been so tasteless. "Here's a question that I can write about: if you weren't an artist, what would you like to be? Or is this the only ambition you've ever had?"

He laughed and sat down, stretched largely, then turned to look at her. "A rodeo star, that's what I really would have liked to be. I'd like to ride a Brahma bull in the stock show in January. Maybe win a big silver belt buckle as best all-around cowboy. Now, that's success!"

Karen sat up, annoyed. He was teasing her. "That sounds fascinating, just fascinating, for a city boy. I'll ask an easier question. What do you think about the work you're doing now? How do you feel about your painting?"

He lifted his arms and laced his fingers behind his head, stared at the painting for a moment, then looked at Karen. "The same way I 'feel about' my women. With my fingers. Would you like me to 'feel about' you?"

"Be serious," she protested. "This is important."

"I'm tired of your questions, and I'm hungry.

Let's eat." He got up and washed his hands after he had covered his paint, then unpacked his backpack.

As they sat on the blanket eating cheese, French bread and sipping a fruity wine, Karen said, "By the way, Nita came to see me. She told me she was sorry for the way she spoke to me last Saturday. She made me promise to let you know she had been nice, and that I had forgiven her." She looked inquiringly at Lee.

He stared out over the valley toward the gold-smudged hills. "Her mouth isn't disciplined," he replied, then glanced at her. "It runs in the family."

Karen fiddled with her wineglass. "She told me a little about your childhood."

Abruptly, Lee got up and began clearing up the remains of lunch. He didn't answer until he had uncovered his palette and taken his position in front of the painting.

"That's not a period in my life I care to remember," he said, and added color to the woman's face. Her mouth came to life in a few simple strokes. Then he sat down on the chair and stared at his work. "I suppose the experience left me cautious and angry," he added.

"How do you handle the anger?" Karen asked, lying on her stomach watching him. "Or is it gone?"

He pointed the palette knife at the picture. "This painting is subdued, she's a subdued lady, but when I paint what I choose, it's generally turbulent. Painting is my escape valve." He looked at Karen. "No, I don't suppose the anger is completely gone, but I've aged and mellowed, developed controls. It isn't possible to erase an unhappy childhood, only to understand it." He raised his eyebrows. "Satisfied, Hunter?"

It was clear he didn't want to talk about it. She nodded and turned over to lie on her back, staring up at the sky. Lee wiped his hands and knife on a rag, then walked over to lie down beside her, propped on an elbow, his head on his hand to look down into her face. She laughed and wiped a smear of paint off his cheek. "Do you always paint yourself along with the canvas?" She rubbed her finger on the blanket.

"I throw myself into my work," he said, closing his eyes lazily.

Karen studied his face, the well-formed bones under smooth, tan skin, his graceful, jutting nose, the curve of his jaw, his lips, faintly pink and pulsing with life and controlled passion. Her eyes drifted down to the muscle in the arm supporting his head, round and strong with a tracing of a vein under the skin. The muscle led into his deep chest, with its crisp, curling black hairs, irresistible nipples. Her lips parted, and her fingers itched to touch him.

"What are you thinking?" he asked, surprising her into a guilty head shake for an answer. He sat up grinning. "You agreed I could ask a question if I let you ask me what you wanted. Now it's my turn." He pulled a knee up and crossed his arms on top of it, his eyes half serious. "It's obvious you're as horny as hell. But what have you got against men?"

"Horny!" Karen sat up indignantly to cover a bright-red blush. "Ho! Don't flatter yourself."

"If you're not, how come you won't look at me?" He ran a fingertip up her thigh, sending a quiver along her nerve endings. "Karen Jane."

"Stop that," she said, jerking her legs away. "And don't call me Karen Jane, I hate it." She turned to glare at him. "Philip Lee." It infuriated her to have been caught in a desire that she refused to acknowledge, mustn't consummate.

Lee moved so fast she didn't have time to react. Snagging both narrow straps of her swim top in his fingers, he jerked her toward his face, his eyes as hard as obsidian. "Don't you ever call me Philip. Not you. Don't ever call me that again." His voice was a harsh whisper and sent chills down her back. "Do you hear me?"

"I hear," Karen whispered, wetting her lips with the tip of her tongue. "I hear, and if you're trying to scare me, you can stop now, because you have."

The expression on his face changed abruptly, first to horror, then to repentant embarrassment. He let her go and rubbed his hand over the back of his neck and through his hair. "I'm sorry," he said bitterly. "So much for my mellow controls. All I can say is that my name, Philip, stands for all the loneliness I felt, when I needed to be loved." He looked at her, his eyes seeking. "I said I understood my childhood, but understanding isn't accepting. I am sorry."

He stood up slowly, to pick up a rock to throw violently out into empty space. "Oh, dammit, Hunter, go home," he said, turning to look at her. "I should never have brought you here. It's too easy to let my guard down on this mountaintop— with you."

Karen stood up. "I'll go home if you want me to, but I'd rather not." She wanted to put her arms around him, comfort him.

"No, I don't want you to go." He came close and put one arm gently around her neck, touching her cheek with his own. Then he pulled back. "But if you had any sense you'd go away and forget about me."

Karen watched him turn his back and walk to the studio. "I've never been praised for my sense," she said. "And you make it awfully hard not to see you—you're always there," she added, feeling perversely rejected.

Lee picked up his palette knife and stared blankly at the painting. "I know it, damn it, and it isn't like me. I should have better sense myself." He glanced at her. "I like you too much, and you have just had a demonstration of what you can expect from me."

"No harm done," Karen said softly. "I'll just remember not to call you bad names."

"You want to stay, then?" he asked.

"I'll have to," she said, lying down on the blanket on her back, shielding her eyes from the sun with an arm. "I'm not pink yet."

She glanced at him. He stood in the doorway, frowning at her. "Get to work, Payne. Your paint is drying out."

He turned back to the painting and sat on the chair, rocking it back, whistling tunelessly through his teeth. After a while, he said, "You didn't answer my question."

"What question?"

"What have you got against men? You have to answer; you owe me, now that you know all about me."

"I haven't anything against men. I like men, a lot, as you so succinctly pointed out earlier."

"As long as they don't get too close?"

"For now, yes," she said. "I can't afford any distractions until I get my career on the road."

She didn't elaborate, and Lee seemed content to let it drop, whistling softly and rocking, occasionally daubing at the canvas.

The sun, hot on Karen's skin, seemed hypnotic. She felt drowsy and intimate, thinking, remembering. "I almost got married once," she offered.

"It was during one of the years when I had to work to earn tuition to go back to school the next term." The whistling didn't stop, and his disinterest encouraged her. "He was a sweet guy . . . name was Peter. I was head over heels, and I thought he was the same. He was in law school."

She smiled wryly to herself. "I had spent quite a bit of time in hospitals during my school years and I'd had to struggle to keep up with my classes. There hadn't been time for social life or friends. Then, when I was twenty, along came Peter. We were like two vines wrapped around each other.

"We had our wedding all planned, the flowers, the cake, the dress. Then we found that we didn't agree on what a wife should be. He had assumed that I would forget about college and concentrate on his career, work to help him finish his education, then be the sort of lawyer's wife who would enhance his status." Karen sat up. Her eyes burned with annoyance. "I couldn't comply. I had to be myself. I couldn't give up my dreams and ambitions. So that was the end of that."

The legs of Lee's chair came down with a thump. He ambled out into the sun and sat down next to Karen. "The man was an idiot," he said.

Karen picked at a scratch on her ankle, a badge for trail climbing. "Not really, just realistic. He's married now and has two children."

"I'd never be able to survive that kind of rejection," he said.

"Yes, you could. You just do it. And quit feeling sorry for me, or you'll have me crying all over you. I can see now that it wouldn't have lasted if we had married. I'm too stubborn and jealous of my own interests."

"So you've sworn off men for life?"

"Not for life." She laughed. "What makes you think men are indispensable?"

Lee looked at her solemnly. "The great masculine ego tells me so. Besides"—he waggled a finger suggestively at her—"did you know your eyes will cross if you do it without a man?"

Karen laughed. "Why don't you go finish your painting, Payne?"

He grinned and went back to his chair, his whistling and his palette knife.

Presently, Karen got up to stand behind him to watch the woman's face take form. She had a healthy pink glow now, still surrounded by green.

Each rock of Lee's chair brought his wide, warm shoulders close to Karen. She wondered how he kept his balance on those two spindly legs.

The portrait lost its fascination as she embraced him with her eyes, the crisp wave of his dark hair, the smooth, tantalizing skin of his neck and arms. Disturbing flushings teased her body.

He had stopped rocking and was balanced immobile on the two chair legs. She knew he was as aware of her presence as she was of his. Her fingers twitched with the need to touch him.

When the desire became too strong to resist, she put her hands lightly on his shoulders, breathlessly feeling the curve where they joined his neck.

He turned his head and rested his cheek on her hand. She jerked away, blushing, suddenly aware of what she had done. She couldn't allow anything to begin between them.

The front legs of his chair came down sharply. "If you're not buying, Hunter," he said in a husky voice, "don't touch the merchandise. You make the natives restless." Although he didn't look at her, all of the attention of his enticing body seemed directed toward her.

She retreated, trembling, to a safe distance and sat down on a battered sofa bed against the far wall. The springs screeched. The sound cried out a message of what they might be doing on those cushions, and she jumped up again.

As if he had the same disconcerting thought, Lee got up and blurted, "Oh, damn! I can't work with you around. I've lost my concentration. We'd better get out of here."

He cleaned his palette and knife, and Karen could see that his hands were shaking and clumsy. Yes, indeed, we'd better get out of here, she agreed silently, and had to consciously forbid her feet to walk to him or her lips to speak of her need for him.

He rushed her irritably down the hill with little grace, and into the Blazer.

In the safety of the truck, she made a few stabs at conversation in an attempt to regain the easy camaraderie they had shared. But when he answered her attempts with only a grunt or a grudging word, she retreated to her side of the seat to frown out the window in hurt silence.

After he had dropped her abruptly in front of her house, she looked after the Blazer until it had disappeared. Then she continued to stare down the empty street, torn between regret that she hadn't let their passion bring them together, and a feeling that she had escaped the most explosive peril.

Finally, when she trudged unhappily up to her front door, she had made a decision.

It had been four days since Karen had seen Lee, four days since she had decided to terminate the tenuous connection that had begun to develop between them.

For the first couple of days, she'd felt a leaden lump of remorse for the necessity that it had to be so. And for the next few days, she had begun to churn with anger because he hadn't come to see her; not a word, a call or a note. The least he could do was have the common decency to get in touch so she could put an end to this budding affair.

She sat at her desk, brooding and staring into space. She'd never met anyone like Lee in her constricted, ordered life. She'd always known where she was going and what she wanted to do, but now since she had so naively allowed him to invade her life, nothing seemed simple. She had developed itches and twitches that couldn't be scratched. How could she work intelligently when half the time she was off in a daydream about muscular thighs, laughing black eyes and . . . the rest?

With a deep sigh, she mentally counted on her fingers, for the hundredth time, the reasons she couldn't see Lee again.

He had no respect whatever for her time and wishes, dragging her off whenever he felt like it, no matter how she protested.

And he made fun of her when she tried to be

serious. Frowning, she became angrier when she thought about it. Plainly, she was only a diversion to him, amusing for the moment.

Which led to those women of his. She had no intention of ever eating the sour grapes of jealousy. Never.

Her most important argument was that she would let herself care too much, and he would treat their relationship like a sideshow. He'd take her up on a carnival ride into ecstasy, then drop her like a used-up Fourth of July sparkler when he was tired of her. She'd be left to fizzle and die. Her eyes flashed anger, imagining the pain. No, sir. That wasn't for her.

A good example was this last Saturday, she thought, her lips turning white at the edges with hurt pride. They had had a lovely time, at least she had, and she had told him things she hadn't meant to say to anyone. They had been close. Then, afterwards, he'd dumped her off like so much excess baggage, and he hadn't taken a minute to call since. Oh, no, not the great P. Lee Payne. He expected her to wait patiently until the next time he crooked his finger at her; then she was supposed to run after him like a stupid puppy dog.

She unclamped her furious fingers from the windowsill and turned around. She simply had to quit thinking about him and get on with the work she was paid to do.

"Wow! You look like a thundercloud."

Karen jumped at Lee's voice as if she'd been struck by a bolt of lightning that accompanied the thundercloud. He was leaning in her doorway and he had been there for some time. "Do you always have to sneak up on me like that?" she demanded angrily. "Can't you knock or speak or something, to let me know you're there? What are you doing here?" she snapped, forgetting she had been berating him in her mind for *not* being here. She felt as if he had been trespassing on her most private thoughts.

Lee stiffened and stood up straight. "I'm beginning to wonder what I'm doing here myself. What lit your fuse?" He reached up to push his battered hat down over his forehead, shielding his eyes.

Karen suddenly realized he used that hat as protection, to hide his feelings. The anger ebbed. "I'm sorry, Lee. I've been trying to work out a problem, and it's frazzling my nerves a little." A lot, she thought, especially with him in her little office. This wasn't going to be easy.

The hat got nudged up a tentative inch. He walked over to sit on the desk, which she'd retreated behind. "Anything I can help with?"

Karen shrugged noncommittally. "What can I help *you* with?" she asked. "You must have had something on your mind, seeing that I'm graced with your presence."

He frowned slightly at her formality. "I came to ask if you'd like to drive down to New Mexico with me this weekend." His voice sounded as if he wasn't sure, after his reception.

She shook her head slowly.

He crossed his arms over his chest, the muscles under his rolled up sleeves bulging tensely. "I've got several paintings in a gallery in Taos, and a bunch more in Santa Fe. The tourist season is over, so I've got to bring my babies home. They'll be in a show here in Denver in a couple of weeks. I thought it might be sort of fun if you kept me company." He watched her warily from under the hat brim, gauging her reaction.

Karen shook her head again, her stomach twisting into a knot. She had the opportunity to put an end to this, but she didn't want to do it. "I can't, Lee. I'm sorry."

A few moments of silence. "Why?"

"Because I don't want to. I've been honest with you—I've never led you to believe I wanted to get involved. And I don't want to. I like you, but let's not go any further." She took a deep breath. "It's been an interview, that's all. I've got the material I need for the article, and there isn't any reason for us to see each other again. I don't think I have to tell you how much I appreciate what you've done for me."

She had never seen his face so dark, with the lines around his mouth and between his brows deepening into crevices. "I imagined something else might be happening between us," he said harshly.

A thrill of doubt twitched through Karen. She glanced at the fists he had made of his hands and forced herself to say, "I like you, I really do, but an affair would never work between us."

She dropped her eyes to her own tightly clasped hands. Surely he wasn't as upset as he looked. She had been so certain he hadn't been serious. Could she have been wrong? Conflicting emotions began to churn within her. She looked up hesitantly.

His black eyes bored into her own confused brown ones. Then he spat an obscenity and twisted off the desk to come around toward her. She jumped up, her breath catching in her throat. He looked as if he meant to throttle her.

When she tried to sidestep him, his fingers dug into the soft flesh of her upper arm, and he pulled her around toward him. Both of his arms went around her, so strong and tight that she had to gasp for breath. She twisted and struggled to escape, but she was helpless against his strength.

Held against him, her breasts flattened against his chest, thighs against thighs, her body gloried in the joy of touching him, but there was no tenderness in his embrace.

With one hand, he pulled her chin up so that she had no choice but to look into the anger in his face. His mouth came down on hers, and she pushed against him with her hands. If she didn't get away instantly, she'd be lost. But it was like pushing against a rock wall.

His lips softened then, and the steel in his arms melted. His mouth caressed hers, and his tongue touched the sensitive inner surface of her upper lip. She could have pulled away now, but she didn't. Her arms slipped up over his chest and curled around his neck. Her body arched tightly against his.

Though her mind was incapable of thought, every other inch of her knew that this was where she belonged, in his arms, as a part of him. The Fourth of July rocket she had feared, went off inside of her with an explosion of sparks.

His sweet musky-male scent enveloped her seductively. The taste of his mouth against hers satisfied any appetite she had ever known but opened up a whole new spectrum of hungers. She wanted to sample every part of him.

Then he lifted his head and dropped the arms that had been holding her. As he tried to draw back, she tightened her arms around his neck and pressed against him. She couldn't bear to be separated from him, not just yet. Not when she had only begun to know him.

He reached up, forced her arms away and stepped back. The hardness had left his face. Now there was only a heart-wrenching, icy expressionlessness there. "That was something for you to remember me by," he said coldly. "And don't worry, I won't bother you again."

Karen felt that she might fall; he had liquified the strength in her limbs with his kiss. She lifted her hand and opened her mouth to cry out to him, but she couldn't speak around the fullness in her throat. All she could manage was a choked, pleading, "Lee . . ."

Then he turned his back, and with three strides of his long legs, P. Lee Payne walked out of Karen's office and out of her life.

She watched his stiff, hurt form disappear through the door and knew that she had been wrong. He hadn't been amusing himself at her expense. He had been ready to care deeply for her.

She felt blindly for her chair and dropped into it, pressing her hands to her face. Tears ran down between her fingers. She also knew that his pride wouldn't allow him to trust her again.

For once, she had accomplished exactly what she had set out to do, in this case to make a clean break with Lee Payne. But all she felt was a terrible, bitter disappointment. It was then that she realized she loved him with every fiber in her body.

The only thing she wanted at this moment was to be able to snatch back every word she had said to him before he had kissed her. But that wasn't possible; he would never listen.

She picked up the crystal paperweight and

pressed it against her cheek . . . "Why can't I ever do anything right?" she demanded of the empty room.

After a long period of silent self-reproach, she took the folder of notes about Lee out of her desk drawer and read through them, with a deep, uncertain frown on her face.

Seven

The days passed, one after another, just as if the earth hadn't turned inside out, as if Karen's world hadn't turned dull and empty. Pride kept her from running to Lee. The look on his face when he had left, haunted her. She had hurt him, and he wouldn't forgive her easily.

In her heart, she knew that all of the reasons she had enumerated before snuffing out her connection with Lee were still valid. But deeper in her heart, she knew irrevocably that she would leap into any kind of emotional danger to be with him again, to feel his lips on hers in love.

A week of longing passed before she could bring herself to reopen the file of notes she had written about him. Each word, each print of his paintings and art photos wrenched the most tender core of her being. She had lost any interest in using the article about him to raise herself in her career, but it seemed to her that if she could write about him with respect and love, cataloging his life and sensitivity with tact and tenderness, he might see it as a message of her feeling.

As she struggled to develop the article, Karen began to see that a large part of his life was missing—the part that must have been the most important. Somewhere between the time he had been an unhappy child and when he had gone into photography, someone must have touched his life to direct his artistic talents.

She leaned on her desk, chewing her pencil, trying to remember a bit of knowledge that eluded her. Then she remembered Nita, in the bar, mumbling in her sentimentality about Lee's foster family. Tillson. Marty and Luther Tillson.

Restlessly, Karen got up to pace her office. Did she dare to contact them? As soon as the possibility of seeing those people had occurred to her, it became a compulsion. Her heart broke to think of the child Lee, lonely and neglected. She had to know what had happened later.

But how? She couldn't simply call and ask to talk to the Tillsons. Could she? She rushed to her desk for the telephone book.

Her fingers trembled so, she could hardly turn the pages. Then, she found the name. They were listed!

Hesitantly, she picked up the phone, even touched the dial. Then she put it down, frowning. They'd never agree to see her. What reason could she give?

What if she dropped in, claiming to be an old friend of Lee's? She discarded that idea with a self-mocking smile. She'd already tried that one, and look at what it had gotten her.

Chewing on her pencil, Karen stared into space and rocked in her chair, until the nub of a plan began to form. Several times, she tossed it out, mentally, as too crude and devious. But it kept coming back insistently.

Finally, she pulled a map out of her drawer. The Tillsons lived on a country road almost at the base of the foothills, near the mouth of Coal Creek Canyon. She carefully calculated the mileage and the amount of gas it would take to drive there.

With her calculations completed, Karen still frowned. The worst that could happen was that she might have a long hike back to a gas station. She slammed the pencil down on the desk, put away the phone book and tucked the map into her purse. She would do it. She had to know about the rest of Lee's young life.

The weather was clear, but a strong Colorado wind was blowing, late the next morning, when Karen drove out of the city on Highway 72 with the arrow on the gas gauge of her VW below empty. First she located the Tillsons' house on a country road, then she drove up and down another road, within a mile of the house but out of sight, until the car sputtered and died, its gas tank dry.

Now that she'd done it, she began to have second thoughts. Her scheme seemed as transparent as the windshield she stared through. She finally let go of the steering wheel and picked up her purse. She had come this far; she might as well go the rest of the way.

The wind hit her like a solid wall as she stepped out of the car, straight from the canyon, pelting her with gravel and dust picked up along the way.

She hunched down and trudged up the road. The walk was half a mile long, but it seemed more like ten miles by the time she turned into the driveway.

The Tillsons' house was a sprawling ranch style, not new but neatly kept, with white siding and gray shutters. The wind grabbed at the fall flowers in the beds in front. There were a couple of sheds and a large fenced field in back, with several horses backed up against the force of the wind, their heads drooping, manes and tails whipping.

The door opened at her knock, as if she had been expected. A small woman in her seventies reached out to draw Karen in, her white hair lifting in the wind. "Come in, come in. I saw you walking up the drive," she said. "You poor thing, you look as if you've been torn apart. What are you doing out walking on a day like this?" The voice was unquestionably welcoming, clear and mellow despite the woman's age.

Karen tried to smooth the tangles in her hair. "I'm sorry to bother you, but I've run out of gas," she said, as she had rehearsed. "I wonder if I can use your telephone to call someone to bring me some?" She breathed a sigh of thanksgiving for the warm, motherly person before her. "My name is Karen Hunter," she added, with the sudden thought that this might not be Marty Tillson.

It was. "And I'm Marty Tillson. You don't need to call for gas. My husband can give you a gallon or so." She ushered Karen insistently through the house. "You just sit down at the table, there, and I'll get you a cup of coffee. You must be exhausted." Marty hustled about the kitchen, reaching for cups and setting out a platter of rolls and cookies as if Karen were a welcome guest rather than the intruder she was, chattering about the wind and the weather. "Luther will be in in a minute. He'll take care of your car; don't you worry. I'm more than happy to have company."

The coffee smelled heavenly, and the cinnamon rolls were homemade. Karen combed her hair into some semblance of order and sat down at the table.

"I hope you don't mind sitting in the kitchen," Marty said, "but we spend most of our time here in the back of the house. It's more homey. We always have, especially when we had the boys."

"It's wonderful," Karen said, sighing from down deep. She bit into a roll, the spice and butter delectable on her tongue. She couldn't have asked for a more perfect home for Lee.

The back door opened with a blast. A tall, rangy man came in, buffeted by the wind, a sweat-stained felt cowboy hat jammed down over his forehead, his face lined and creased with a lifetime of living, laugh lines and worry lines intermingling. He closed the door and took off the hat to nod and smile at Karen. "Company?" he asked with a questioning look at Marty. Karen smiled, realizing Lee had patterned himself after this man.

Marty explained Karen with cluckings of sympathy.

"No problem, little lady," Luther drawled, "I've got a gallon of gas in a can out back. I'll have you back in business in no time. Unless you've got one of those monster gas-guzzlers that can't make it across the street on a gallon."

"No"—Karen laughed—"just a little bug." She got up and looked out the window. She pointed out the spot of yellow in the distance over the flat.

Luther put his hat on over his thinning gray

hair, jamming it down in preparation for the onslaught of the wind.

"More coffee?" Marty poured another cup, then
sat down across from Karen. A big, fluffy gray cat
climbed onto her lap.

Karen looked around the room, trying to imagine a young Lee here. A painting on the wall across
from her caught her attention. It was certainly one
of Lee's, an early one, but without the dynamic
command of the others she had seen. "That's
beautiful," she said, pointing.

Marty turned to look. "Yes, isn't it? One of our
boys did that." She turned back toward Karen.
"Lee Payne. Do you know him?" She obviously
assumed everyone knew Lee Payne.

"Yes," Karen said as objectively as she could
manage, but she felt a blush creep into her cheeks.

Marty didn't miss it. Her eyes sharpened, twin-
kling, and for a few seconds, she studied Karen,
inspecting her inside and out, it seemed. "Do you
know him well?"

"Oh, no. No. I've just talked to him a few times.
Business," she ended weakly.

Marty laughed. "He's grown up to be an attrac-
tive man, hasn't he?" She laughed again. "He's
our foster son, you know, our last one. But we've
always felt he was more like our own."

Marty gave Karen another penetrating look. "Did
you know he went to the University of Colorado at
Boulder on scholarships?" Karen shook her head.
"But enough about that. Tell me about you. Are
you married?"

Karen shook her head and found herself talking
to Marty as she would to an old friend. Marty
must have been a marvelous foster mother. She
didn't have a threatening bone in her body, just

warm friendliness and interest. It was difficult to keep Lee out of the conversation.

When Luther drove the car into the yard and came in, Marty and Karen were solid friends. Later, Karen drove reluctantly back to the office.

By the time Karen left work that afternoon at five, the wind had blown itself out as mysteriously as it had arisen, leaving the air pristine and clear, charged with an exhilarating energy.

When she walked into her house, the only sign of life was the sound of music on the radio in the kitchen. "Mom?" she called from the foot of the stairs. "I've got a headache. I'm going to take a nap, okay?"

There was no answer, and Karen was just as glad. She had no desire for conversation. Each step she climbed toward her bedroom sent electric currents of pain up her neck and into her head. At least it was Friday. She might just sleep through the whole miserable weekend.

Walking like a robot, she moved toward her bedroom. Then stopped short to stare open-mouthed at her doorway. First a foolish grin spread over her face, then a look of bewilderment and anxiety.

She inspected the clothes hanging on three hangers from the door frame. A pair of tan gabardine trousers, western cut, flared at the bottom, with creases sharp enough to cut bread. She ran her fingers over a silky, pale-blue shirt. The third hanger sported a beaded, fringed vest of soft velvety suede. Her pulse had speeded to overload. Oddly, her headache had disappeared.

She couldn't explain the presence of the clothes.

Was Lee here? Surely something should have tipped her off when she walked in. Her mother hadn't answered when she called. Maybe they had gone out somewhere. She knew her mother and Lee liked each other, and she supposed he wouldn't cut Elsie out of his life too. The thought that popped into her head made her muscles tense. Could he know she had visited the Tillsons? No, she decided, it hadn't been an important enough incident in their life to report.

She debated what to do. Hide until the clothes disappeared? Go out and call a girlfriend to arrange to spend the evening out? She pursed her lips. Take the bull by the horns and face him?

The first thing she had to do was find her mother and see what this was all about.

She ran back downstairs and into the kitchen.

"I thought you were going to take a nap," Elsie said, looking up innocently, holding a hand of five playing cards against her chest. "How is your headache?" She gestured to a tall frosty glass that looked like it had been sitting in the freezer, judging from the cloud of cold steam around it. Then, "Call!" she declared jubilantly, glancing at her cards. "Let's see what you've got."

Karen stood frozen in the doorway.

"Hah!" Lee said, grinning maliciously. He spread his cards on the table with a flick of his wrist. "Three jacks. See if you can beat that."

"Sorry," Elsie said, "but this looks like a straight." She raked in the macaroni they were using for poker chips.

"Damn," Lee said, looking up at Karen. "She's into me for five dollars."

Karen tried to read his face. She could see nothing. She walked in and sat down, picking up the glass. "It serves you right for trying to con an old lady," she said, surprised that her voice worked. If only she could see into his mind. She watched him deal out the cards.

His hat was pushed way down over his eyebrows, so, if that was an indication of his feelings, he wasn't comfortable either. But he seemed very intent on the card game. She studied the hair at the back of his head as if it might tell her something. It was black as night in the shadow of the hat and curled slightly at the back of his neck where it touched the blue frayed collar. It was charming, but it had no answer.

Karen sipped from the glass. There was something more than lemonade in it. She wondered suspiciously why they were softening her up and scraped at the frost on the glass with a fingernail. Whatever happened, it was heaven to be close to Lee again, just to look at him. Even if he didn't seem to take much interest in her. She wished she didn't always have to fight the impulse to touch him. Elsie and Lee picked up their cards and stared at each other poker-faced.

"By the way," Karen said casually, "what are those clothes doing on my bedroom door? Salvation Army pickup?" She didn't like being ignored.

"I'll stand pat," Elsie said, clutching her cards to her body.

"Dealer takes two," Lee said, and did, frowning into his hand. "A gallery is opening a new show. I've got a section in it. Big reception tonight. I'm supposed to be there; hence the clothes. Had to store them somewhere."

"Kind of a kinky outfit, isn't it?" At least he had spoken to her.

"Wait until you see the turquoise jewelry that

goes with it. I've got an image to live up to. My public expects a certain amount of kinky glamour from an artist, don't you know?" He contemplated Elsie's raise of two curved macaroni, then he bunched his hand. "Hell, I fold. What have you got?"

"Wouldn't you like to know?" Elsie put her hand face down on the deck and took the pasta.

Karen looked at her mother's cards, then at Lee's, and laughed.

Lee muttered and put the deck of cards in its box, then he turned toward Karen, leaning one elbow on the table, the other on the chair back, and clasped his hands. "How's your headache?"

Karen took a sip from her drink and looked at him warily. "Better."

"It's enough to give anyone a headache, running out of gas and all."

She choked on a swallow, coughing and sputtering. She tried to think of something to say, but nothing came to her.

"Hunter," he said, "you come up with the most juvenile, simplistic schemes. And the wonder of them is that they work."

She turned sideways in her chair to stare intently at the refrigerator. She knew her mother was laughing silently, but she didn't know what Lee felt. "How did you find out?" she asked hesitantly.

"Marty couldn't wait to get on the phone and report in," Lee answered. "You're the most exciting thing that's happened to her in months, maybe years."

Karen took a quick look at him. He wasn't smiling, but he didn't look fierce. "Are you mad?" she asked.

"I frothed at the mouth until she told me to shut up and listen."

Karen let out a breath she had been holding and turned back to the table to take a gulp from her glass.

"You dummy," he said. "She knew all about you before you set foot in her door. I'd told her what was going on." He laughed as Karen put a hand over her forehead and breathed out sharply through her nose. "But she was willing to go along with your little game. Enjoyed it, in fact. She's just about as gullible as you are."

"And you're not angry?" Karen felt hot with embarrassment.

"Maybe I'm a little naive myself. I thought you had gone to snoop for that cursed article of yours, but Marty assured me you didn't ask question one about me." He grinned. "You really missed your chance—she would have told you every move I've made since I was fifteen. She loves to talk about me." He frowned at her. "You found yourself a cheering section out there, you know. Although I can't imagine why, little sneak that you are. The only problem that Marty can see is that you're too good for me. She gave me all sorts of instructions on how to behave with you." He shrugged and made a face. "But I told her to forget it, you aren't interested in me."

Karen glanced at Elsie, who was gazing into the distance, making it clear that she hadn't the slightest interest in the conversation. "Well," Karen said, for lack of anything more intelligent to say.

"Why *did* you go see Marty and Luther?" Lee asked, his eyes steady on her from under the hat.

Karen took a sip, shrugged, raised her eyebrows,

then she laughed. "Because I'm interested in you."
The worst understatement she had ever made.

The hat came up, thumbed back to let a lock of
dark hair fall on his forehead. "Want to go to the
art show with me tonight?"

"I thought you'd never ask." Her heart flew and
sang. "What should I wear?"

Elsie gave an enormous sigh and rejoined the
conversation. "I've got your things laid out on
your bed. You go do something about your hair;
you look like you've stuck your finger in a light
socket."

Karen put her hands to her head. Her hair felt
like wire from the punishment it had taken from
the wind. "Speak about conspiracies," she said,
and got up.

Lee reached out and touched her arm, looking
up at her. "Wear your hair loose tonight, for me?"

Karen nodded and ran upstairs to shower and
shampoo her hair, to wash away the ecstatic tears
she didn't want anyone to see.

After they'd eaten dinner, Karen dressed with
all the excitement of a girl going on her first date.
She slipped into a white satin halter top that left
her shoulders and back bare, and plunged over
the golden skin between her breasts. She tucked
the top into a long black velvet skirt with a wide
band, which showed off her small waist. She studied her figure in the mirror, pleased, and fastened
a couple of gold chains around her neck.

She wanted to be perfect tonight. She knew she
wasn't sophisticated-looking like a fashion model,
but she would be happy if she looked pretty.

Brushing her hair one more time, she critically
inspected her makeup. It was subtle, the way she
liked it, with a blend of rose and beige over her

eyelids, and a hint of green to bring out the gold in her brown eyes, just a touch of coral lip gloss and nail polish to match and blusher to lift her cheekbones.

It pleased her that the sun had streaked her hair, framing her face with ripe wheat, waving and silky, falling to below her shoulders.

Slipping her feet into black shoes with narrow straps, Karen picked up a white brocade evening bag and floated down the stairs.

When she saw Lee's face, she knew she had achieved the effect she wanted.

He came close and touched a soft wave of her hair with his finger, then stood back to look at her. "Lovely," he said softly. "Like an elegant waif." He let his fingers trail down her bare shoulder.

She gave a delicious shiver and looked him over. "I feel more like a wren with a peacock."

He looked down at himself. The pale blue shirt was open to mid-sternum, with a turquoise pendant nesting in the hair on his chest. A bigger piece of blue stone decorated the belt that ornamented his snug pants. The fringed vest fit his chest like a glove, and his dark-brown boots shone like mirrors. He had left his hat on the table in the kitchen. "Not a peacock, a rooster, and not a wren, a magpie. A black-and-white cheeky magpie."

She laughed, and they went out to climb into a silver-gray Porsche. Karen had been right: he did have something fancier for his special women. She breathed a contented sigh and ran her hand over the plush maroon seat. Special.

Eight

The Martingale Gallery stood snobbishly apart from the other buildings in an exclusive shopping center in a southern suburb of Denver. Trimmed with black and chrome, its lobby windows glowed with the soft light of chandeliers. Karen peered at the windows apprehensively as she walked toward the door beside Lee. "Are you sure I look all right?" she asked.

Lee smiled and took her arm. "You look beautiful. Don't let anyone intimidate you—they're all show, just like me."

A receptionist recognized Lee and greeted them warmly, waving them into the gallery.

The soft lighting reflected on the jewelry and gowns bedecking the women, who milled sociably with their more sedate male companions, who wore dinner jackets or dressy western attire. Soft music, muted conversation and discreet laughter floated about the central room.

The paintings were displayed in separate elaborately lighted rooms, segregated as to artist and style.

The attention of the gathering polarized as Lee and Karen walked into the room. A milling crowd of well-wishers surrounded them, vying for recognition. Lee held Karen's arm protectively, accepting the deference of the crowd with unexpected poise. Karen smiled, murmuring answers and making small talk, bewildered by the interest she aroused whenever Lee introduced her. These people seemed familiar with her, and curious.

A young waiter held a tray in front of her. She took a stemmed glass and sipped champagne, then eased herself away from Lee and out of the crowd.

Wandering around the display rooms, Karen studied the paintings. Some of the signatures she recognized; others were new to her. One room held the muted Indian symbolism of Charlie Whitehorse. He had also done several canvases of Indian life. The faces in those paintings were compelling and mysterious.

"Oh, there you are." Lee appeared beside her. "I thought I had lost you. Have you seen mine yet?" He looked at her inquiringly as if he were nervous.

She shook her head. "I'm saving the best till last. Why don't you give me a tour of them?"

Before they could leave, a voice, high and musical, demanded Lee's attention. "Darling!" A young woman came between Lee and Karen. Karen moved back to stand against the wall and watch. The woman, slender and almost as tall as Lee, wrapped him in her arms, a musky perfume wafting around her as she moved in a flowing dress that seductively accentuated every angle and curve in her body. She didn't kiss him—it didn't seem necessary—she ground her pelvis against his, murmuring in his ear.

Karen tapped her empty glass against her teeth and watched angrily. The girl was exquisite, with masses of auburn hair coiled high on her head over a flawless, carnal face.

Lee's hands made a brown contrast against the white material covering the swell of her hip. He gave her his intense, dark-eyed concentration, but when he looked up for a momentary check on Karen, she saw a glint of humor.

Lee might be amused, but Karen wasn't. She put her empty glass down on a table with an angry click. Before she could disappear in the crowd, Lee had disentangled himself and caught her. "Hey, you look stormy. You aren't jealous, are you?"

"Why ever should I be?" she asked, seething.

He looked back at the girl, who had joined a couple of people in front of a painting. "That's Chastity," he said. "She's harmless—just another old friend."

"I'll just bet she is, a very close old friend," Karen said acidly. "Chastity?"

"A name, not a statement." Lee laughed and led her away. Starting at the left side of his own exhibit, Lee explained to Karen the background of each painting and what he had tried to capture.

Every third picture was a photographic print, its subdued black and white contrasting with the color of the paintings. The photographs were candid portraits of people going about their ordinary lives, their emotions captured in an unguarded moment. The sadness, anger and elation Karen saw reflected in them made her feel as if she'd trespassed on their privacy.

Another man joined them. Lee greeted him with an exuberant hug, slapped him on his back, then let him go and pulled Karen forward. "Karen, meet my friend Charlie Whitehorse."

Karen nodded, speechless, and put her hand hesitantly in the paw Charlie extended.

"Don't let me frighten you," he said, his grin a flash of white in a dark face. "The costume is mostly show. I have to outdazzle our friend, here, don't you see?"

Karen looked him over. "I think you've done it." Charlie had coarse black hair pulled back in the Navaho style. A loose midnight-blue velvet shirt hung over his hips, cinched in the middle with a belt of hammered silver medallions. An elaborate silver-and-turquoise necklace almost covered his chest.

"Lee is the urban competition," Charlie was saying. "And I'm just a poor country boy from Santa Fe, so I have to try harder. I do native American art." He looked at her face intently. "So you're the one. Interesting."

"I'm the one who what?"

Charlie looked at Lee thoughtfully. "She hasn't seen it yet?" Lee shook his head and glanced at Karen.

"Well, well," Charlie said. "Maybe you'd better go charm your admiring public, my cowardly friend. I'll show Karen your pictures."

Lee looked relieved and left. Karen stared after him, frowning suspiciously.

Charlie led Karen through the burlap-covered dividers on which Lee's paintings were displayed, explaining each one technically, describing the use of color and the intended effect. He talked nonstop, in a cultured, crisp manner that fascinated her, it seemed so inconsistent with his appearance. She loved listening to him, and she knew much of what he was saying would be valuable for the article about Lee.

Then, at the very end of the display room, mounted by itself on the end wall, in the place of honor, she saw the picture.

Karen stopped short and stared at it. At first, she cringed in embarrassment, then she swelled with anger, her eyes blazing. "That miserable fink," she whispered.

Charlie put two fingers against his lips and stared at the picture. "You don't like it?" he asked artlessly, transferring his attention to Karen. "It seems quite charming to me."

"He hung that here to humiliate me," she said. "He said he wasn't angry, but he was, and this is his way of getting back at me." Her fists clenched. "Lord, I could kill that man."

Charlie raised his eyebrows over his deep-set brown eyes, then squinted, creasing the coppery skin around his eyes. "He has caught the essence of your loveliness—" he said tentatively.

"It's disgusting!" Karen snapped.

The photograph, softened and misted by darkroom techniques, showed her own face, dreamy and heavy-eyed, gazing wistfully at the front of a man's blue-jeaned pelvis, lips parted and moist. Karen could distinctly remember Lee telling her to lick her lips as he had positioned and posed her in his studio on that day when he had talked her into sitting for him. And she could remember looking at his fly.

She pressed her fist to her forehead, muttering angrily about her stupidity and his arrogance, looking at the picture with disbelief and mortification. A glint of light reflected off the tab of the zipper peeking out of the fly of his jeans, holding the girl's, her, attention in adolescent desire. The background was a fantasy fog, like an erotic dream.

Karen whirled around, startling Charlie. "I've got to get out of here. Where can I find a telephone to call a cab?"

Charlie took her arm and steered her back through the display room and out into the front of the gallery. Karen imagined everyone was staring at her, laughing about the juvenile display she had made of herself. She dropped her eyes and walked stoically beside Charlie. Lee was nowhere in sight. Luckily for him, she thought, because she'd have killed him cheerfully, in full view of every person in the room.

Charlie took her into an office at the back of the building and closed the door. He sat down behind the desk and found a telephone book, while Karen paced furiously back and forth in front of the desk.

"The picture is quite beautiful, really," he said thoughtfully, rustling the pages ineffectively, "although I'll have to admit it might have been tactless to surprise you with it."

"Tactless? Tactless?" Karen stopped and glared at him. "He did it on purpose to teach me a lesson for interfering in his life." She went back to her pacing. "Well, that's one lesson I've learned, but good! I hope I never see him again as long as I live!"

Charlie leaned back and crossed his arms over

his chest, the telephone book open on his knees. "That's probably a wise decision. Lee Payne is a difficult man. He'd run any woman a ragged race. You're better out of it. It's wiser to opt for a nice, sane, quiet life."

Karen stopped and looked at him. "I thought that you were his friend."

"I am. I know him as well as anyone does. Friendship is one thing; a man-and-woman relationship is another. A woman wants a nice, predictable man. Lee will never be that." He thumbed through the phone book again.

He looked up at her. "What *did* you expect from him?"

Karen frowned thoughtfully. "I don't really know." She touched the gold chain at her neck idly. "He took me by storm, I guess. I can't explain what I feel." She hit her forehead with her fist. "Oh, I wish he hadn't done this."

Charlie put the phone book aside. "Are you absolutely certain he hung the picture to spite you? It seems a lovely, lovely punishment. I'm sure if he had been vindictive, he would have made you appear ugly or drawn out any number of more unflattering emotions than that of an ingenue."

Karen considered that. She couldn't deny the truth in his words. "But why, then?"

"Our Lee is a romantic, but a timid one. He bleeds very easily. It's quite unusual for him to publicly exhibit a personal interest. He feels much more at ease with women who pursue him. In their case, he isn't chancing rejection. He can do the finishing himself, with nothing to gamble on."

He looked at Karen for a moment. "I take it, by your reaction to the picture, that you haven't slept together?"

Karen shook her head and colored slightly.

"Interesting. The picture, if I know Lee as well as I think I do, is a statement that he is pleased you are attracted to him and that he sees you as a sensual and desirable woman. But he's afraid."

"Afraid!" Karen repeated.

"As I said, he bleeds easily, and profusely."

Karen thought about it, her anger completely dissipated.

"Shall I call the cab now?" Charlie asked, opening the phone book. "I think I've found the page."

"It took you awhile, didn't it?" Karen smiled. "No, I think not. I'm going to have another look at that picture."

Charlie stood up and smiled. "I hoped you might. And Karen, if you ever visit Santa Fe, come and see us. My wife would like you. She's particularly fond of Lee."

Karen nodded. She walked back through Lee's display and stood for several minutes in front of the picture, looking at it objectively, and even wondered if she truly was that beautiful.

When she went back to the central room, Lee still wasn't in evidence, so she found the woman's lounge and sat in a padded chair to think about what Charlie had told her. It didn't seem possible that Lee was so seriously interested in her.

To Karen's annoyance, the door opened soon after she had settled herself. She had hoped for a few minutes of privacy to compose herself, and this woman was the last she would have chosen for company.

Chastity, an unforgettable name—and woman— moved with sensual grace to study herself lovingly in the mirror, smoothing a sculptured eyebrow, patting unnecessarily at her perfect hair, eyeing Karen surreptitiously in the glass. Karen had the feeling this encounter wasn't accidental.

Chastity satisfied herself with her appearance, then turned to lean against the vanity and light a cigarette, blowing smoke delicately toward the ceiling. Her eyes recorded and pigeonholed Karen. She smiled slightly, barely curving her full lips. "You have a charming hairstyle," she said. "It reminds me of Alice in Wonderland."

Karen stiffened. So that was the way it was going to be. "It does me too," she answered. "I don't usually wear it this way, but I had a special request tonight."

Chastity's eyes narrowed, revealing that she had gotten Karen's message. "That's an interesting picture of you in Lee's display, quite adolescent. Aren't you swimming a little beyond your depth with him?"

Karen willed herself to control her anger. "I'll agree it is adolescent. Lee seems to be a master at getting the effect he wants."

Chastity smoothed the slinky material over her flat stomach and down long thighs with a dainty red-nailed hand. "You are trespassing on my territory," she said coldly.

"If Lee is your territory," Karen said, smiling sweetly, "I'm sure you will have no trouble holding him."

"I'm not terribly worried; you aren't Lee's type. He likes to be pursued, and I doubt that you have the skill for that." Chastity ran water over the glowing end of her cigarette and threw it into the wastebasket. "If he had known I was available tonight, I would have been with him.

Unfortunately, I wasn't able to get in touch with him."

Karen smoothed her hair. "I'm amazed that you found him so hard to contact," she said, and stood up. "He seems very available to me. Ever since I've met him, he's been under my feet. Whenever I turn around, I bump into him." She smiled. "So nice to have met you, Chastity." Optical ice darts followed her as she walked out the door.

Lee had been looking for her. "I can't keep track of you tonight. Where have you been?"

"Oh, Chastity and I were having a nice little chat."

He grimaced and looked at her apprehensively. "You and Charlie had a 'little chat' too?"

Karen nodded. She had no intention of making anything easy for him. Let him worry. He took a glass from a passing waiter and handed it to her. She accepted it and put it on a table untouched.

Finally he asked, "You saw the picture?"

"I saw the picture." She gazed around at the milling people.

"Well?"

"That's really quite a talent you have for catching people at their most vulnerable, Payne. You pain. I should sue you for defamation of character or invasion of private thoughts, or something like that." She tried to stifle the laugh that bubbled up, and failed.

With a relieved grin, Lee put his arm around her shoulders and leaned in close. "The camera doesn't lie, Hunter. Let's go find Charlie and get out of here."

For the rest of the night, they listened to music in half a dozen different clubs, while Lee and

Charlie traded artist's shop talk and rehashed ancient brawls and romances. Karen listened happily.

It was after twelve o'clock when Lee brought Karen home. Her house was dark and silent.

Inside the door, he took her into his arms, his breath hot and quick on her cheek. Karen turned to him eagerly, putting her arms around him, her hands on the smooth material that covered the hard muscles of his back. His lips were as soft as silk on hers, then hard and demanding. It seemed as if all the blood in her body dropped into her pelvis, making it heavy with urgency. With an explosion of stars, she felt she must be levitating; nothing felt solid. The picture hadn't lied. She wanted him. Now!

The sound of a key in the door behind them broke the spell. "Damn it!" Lee whispered with a trembling voice. "Why don't you get a place of your own?"

"Lee . . . I . . ." Karen forgot what she had wanted to say. The door opened, and she stepped away from him as her mother walked into the dark entry.

When Elsie flipped on the light, she jumped and blinked a couple of times, then looked sheepish. "Oh! Oh, I didn't mean to . . . Should I go out and come in again?" She laughed. "Never mind. I'll just go upstairs. Don't let me bother you."

Lee and Karen laughed softly together. Then Karen said, "I'm hungry. Let's get something to eat."

"Okay," Lee agreed, opening the door. "Where do you want to go?"

"Oh, I don't know. Can you fix me something at your place?" Karen asked.

"I might be able to manage," Lee said, grinning, as he settled her in the silver car.

For once Karen didn't mind the speed. Her desire flew on ahead of her, begrudging every minute and every mile.

Nine

The stars above Lee's front yard blazed like shattered glass strewn across black velvet. A few wispy clouds drifted across the big white moon, turning it on and off. The air felt cold and crisp, and smelled of dew and grass. Karen shivered slightly.

Lee stood behind her and put his arms around her, curling his body around hers. "Want to go in?" he whispered, his breath warm on her cheek.

"Not just yet," she murmured. "It's so beautiful here."

The breeze swirled through the pine trees, moaning softly, spreading the deep, pungent scent. Somewhere in the distance a bird cried, a single warning in the night. It wasn't repeated. Odd little rustlings could be heard in the bushes. Karen tried to peer into the impenetrable darkness, suddenly aware of how much black forest there was. "Are there bears around?" she whispered.

"Nary a one," Lee whispered against her hair. "But there have been a few stories about were-wolves." He nipped the side of her neck with his teeth. "You'd better watch out."

Karen brushed him away and laughed. "It's vampires that bite, you fool. But maybe I do want to go in."

They walked to the door, Karen's hand tight and safe and warm in Lee's, her long velvet skirt whispering across the soft bed of pine needles, her pulse racing with anticipation.

In the house, words seemed hugely unnecessary, or impossible. In the light, in the enormous beamed room, with the bedroom so accessible beyond the balcony, Karen struggled with a paroxysm of shyness.

Lee stood looking at her, still holding her hand, his hair fanned over his forehead from the breeze. He smiled, then laughed softly. "I'll make a fire." The dogs padded sleepily beside him.

Karen watched him make a major ceremony of crumpling paper in the fireplace, laying the logs and scratching matches, charmed because she realized he felt the same shyness that she did, and she hadn't expected it of him.

The paper crackled into flame that ate into the kindling. A whiff of sweet smoke drifted through the room. Karen slipped out of her shoes and joined Lee in front of the fire, digging her toes into the thick, springy carpet, to watch the fire leap up.

He had his hands in his pockets, jingling coins, as he watched her, his eyes as dark as the forest outside, like probes that excited the network of nerves under every inch of her skin. She wanted to throw herself on him, but a fit of timidity seemed to have paralyzed her.

"Well." Lee spoke into the silence, and Karen jumped as if she'd been jabbed. "What do you want to eat?"

"I don't know. What have you got?" Eat? Who wanted to eat?

"I've got a couple of steaks in the freezer," he said, leading her into the kitchen. "It wouldn't take long to broil them."

"Too much trouble," Karen said, "just make something simple." She watched his muscles move under his pants as he walked in front of her, and felt as breathless as if she'd jogged ten blocks.

Lee opened the refrigerator. "Let's check it out, see if there's anything that turns you on."

There is! There is something! She screamed silently. She stood looking sightlessly at the refrigerator shelves, blinking at the bright light. Waves of cold drifted out, chilling her, while Lee stood just behind her with one arm on the refrigerator door and the other hand on top of the icebox. Waves of heat from him scorched her back.

She wished he'd make his advance and put her out of her misery. With his experience, it would have to be sophisticated.

"Let's see," he said, a couple of inches from her ear, his voice deep and sensuous, sending shivers to her fingertips. "There's ham for a sandwich, or a leftover enchilada. I could make some soup. Go to bed with me? An omelet wouldn't be too much trouble."

So much for sophistication. She laughed softly, her worries gone. "Umm-m," she murmured, "I don't think ham. The enchilada looks disgusting, and I don't like eggs or soup."

Lee contemplated that for a few seconds; she could feel him smiling. The vibrations darted between them like heat lightning.

Turning, Karen touched his face, memorizing its shape with her fingers, dark arched brows, his fine nose, his lips, soft and warm, the long thick lashes. She brushed his mouth with a kiss and laughed, a shaky sound. "I expected something more suave from you, Payne," she whispered. "You're offering yourself like something on a platter of cold cuts."

"Hot dish," he disagreed, looking just a little embarrassed. "I've never had to ask before. It's scary. You might say no."

Karen ran her hands down his back to the end of his vest. "Now, why would I say no? You know perfectly well I've hardly been able to keep my hands off you since the first time I saw you." She pulled the vest up and over his head.

He came out grinning and tousle-headed. She dropped the vest and touched the buttons on his shirt. He held her hands. "If you can't control yourself, Hunter," he said, laughing, "we'd better get out of the refrigerator before we burn out the motor."

After that, he took control, just the way she wanted it.

The beams across the ceiling of the living room whirled and swayed as Lee carried her in his strong arms up the stairs. Karen put her arms tightly around his neck and pressed her face into his shoulder, delighting in the sweet vertigo of motion and delicious passion, until he let her slide slowly down his body to stand in the bedroom.

He hit the switches on a console by the bed and

the lights went out, except for the warm orange
flickering glow from the fire.

For a long, timeless minute, they stood looking
at each other, filled with wonder that they were
here, at this magical place.

Lee reached out and put his warm, gentle hands
on either side of her neck. "You're so lovely," he
whispered. "I've waited so long."

Putting her arms around the hard, silk covered
muscles of his back, she murmured, "Oh, Lee,"
but anything else she might have said got blocked
by the thick, hot emotion of love rising in her
breast.

She pressed her craving body against his and
felt his fingers working at the clasp at the back of
her neck and on the zippers at her lower back.
The touch made her moan. Then he pulled away
from her and brought his hands down slowly over
her body lowering the material of her satin halter.
His hands trailed fire down over her breasts and
cupped gently under each. Looking at them with
the eyes of an artist, he found them good and
sighed deeply, his deep chest rising under her
hands.

The velvet of her skirt and the satin whispered
down to lay in a black and white pool around her
feet. She stood, slim and rounded out with desire
for him in a lacy half-slip of the palest apricot.
Shivers of anticipation gave her skin a life of its
own.

When he put his hands on the slip, Karen
stopped him. Instead, she unfastened each button of his shirt, slipping the garment away from
him, letting it fall, its blue joining the black and
white of her clothes. She touched him, wonderingly
tracing each muscle in his chest and down his

arms. Moving close, she brushed her jutting nipples back and forth against the crisp curling hair on his chest.

For a long, breathless moment, they looked into each other's eyes, smoldering black into heated brown, the reflection from the fire down below flickering between them.

Then Lee circled her with his arms, pulling her close. "Oh, darling," he said, his voice husky and hot against her neck. "I need you so much. You don't know what you've been doing to me all this time. You're so special."

They both trembled, deeply serious, lost in the wonder of the moment. "I know what I've done," she whispered into the nest of his shoulder where her face lay. "I haven't made you half as miserable as I've been. I need you and want you, too."

He moved away and reached for the slip covering her and with sudden worry, she stopped him. "I've got scars," she whispered apologetically, her eyes pleading.

"So have I," he answered and the slip fell with the rest, a whisp of panties after it. "You are lovely. Perfect," he said with awe and she knew by the expression on his face that his words were true.

As he teased every mound and curve of her body, she whimpered with delight until he took her into his arms and possessed her mouth, tongue on quivering membrane. A sweet, sweet taste filled her with screams of desire that couldn't be voiced, only born, until . . . His tongue left her lips to burn a trail down the side of her neck, flicking and exploding each cell, every pulse with a fire of longing.

When he drew back, she moaned in protest.

Pulling back the covers on his bed, Lee laid her on the smooth sheet to wait for him.

With his eyes on her full of intense emotion, and with fingers that trembled, he tugged at his boots. Then he peeled off his trousers. Karen watched in a frenzy of hunger as he stripped off his pants. Then she drew him down beside her and they joined with frantic urgency.

"You are fantastic," Lee murmured, touching her cheek with wonder. "I've never known anyone like you. I've never known lovemaking so . . . so completely wonderful!"

She put her hand over his and moved her head to kiss his palm. "If I'm fantastic, it's because of you. It must be the artistic genius in you."

Cuddling her face down against his chest, the hairs tickling her cheek, she listened to his heart slow from a thundering gallop to a steady, reassuring rhythm. Every few minutes, she sighed deeply with total satisfaction and complete happiness. Each time, one of his own sighs would match hers, lifting her head with his breath and dropping it. She laughed softly.

"What's funny?" he murmured, his hand lazily running up and down her back.

Shaking her head slightly, she answered, "Nothing, I'm just happy."

Fire-flame patterns danced on the ceiling and beams overhead, and Lee's fingers traced a similar design on Karen's shoulder, random and mesmerizing. "That was so beautiful, Karen J.," he said, the sound rumbling in his chest under her ear, "and now one mystery is solved. You're no virgin, Hunter. You know too many tantalizing tricks."

"Neither are you, Payne. You know a trick or two yourself." She wound a leg around one of his and nuzzled his shoulder, warm in the circle of his arms. Tracing the pattern of hair that grew down over his stomach, she discovered he was ticklish. He captured her hand and held it.

Another sigh, then an answering one, and Karen smiled. "You might not be the first, but you're the best, and very special," she murmured.

A slight tensing of the muscles under and around her surprised her. He didn't comment. She wondered what had displeased him. "I mean it, you're some kind of neat guy, don't you know that?" She kissed the moist curve of his neck and closed her eyes against his cheek. Again she felt a muscle contract, this time in his jaw, under her forehead. She felt too sleepy and relaxed to wonder about it.

After a while, Karen opened her eyes and pulled herself up. She must have dozed. The fire downstairs had died away to no more than a flicker. "What time is it?" she asked.

"What difference does it make?" Lee asked, pulling his arm out from under her, flexing his fingers.

There was just enough light to see her watch. "It's four o'clock! I've got to go home."

Groaning, Lee reached down and pulled up a blanket, pushing her down and tucking it around her shoulders. "What's wrong with here?"

Karen sat up again, the blanket falling away from her bare breasts. "My mother would never understand."

Lee put his hands under his head and grinned

at her. "Who, Elsie? Don't tell me you have a curfew."

"No, but . . . she just wouldn't understand."

Lee laughed. "Elsie will understand. She's had her own little friendships with men over the years, and it's hard to believe they were playing tiddly winks."

"My mother? Never. No way. She's . . . she's naive."

"No, you're naive. *She*'s a sexy old broad." He pulled his knees up under the blanket, forming twin peaks.

"That's a terrible thing to say, Payne. How would you know if she's had men, when I don't?"

"I asked," he said, grinning irritatingly. "Don't look so scandalized. You're in no position to make judgments." He reached out and cupped her breast with his hand.

Then she had to laugh. "I don't know why I never considered that my mother might need something like what we've just had."

Lee's eyes had closed. Karen yanked the blanket away. "Hey, Payne, you look too comfortable. You said you'd fix me something to eat. I'm hungry now."

"If I do, do you promise to settle down and go to sleep?" He had recaptured the blanket and balled it up against his body.

"Maybe, if I don't think of something more interesting to do." She let her fingers wander over the parts of him that were showing. "But I want to eat first." Her fingers found their way under the blanket.

"You'd better watch it, Hunter, or I won't be in any condition to get close enough to the stove to cook. Don't you have any modesty?" He threw back the blanket and got out of bed.

She treasured his form with her eyes. "No, around you I don't think I do have any modesty. Why? Did you need some?"

"Not especially"—he grinned—"but put on this robe anyway, or you'll freeze your pretty little bottom off."

With a wide, pleased smile he watched her put on the oversized dark-blue velour robe, bunching it around her middle and rolling up the sleeves, then he found another for himself, and they went downstairs, their arms around each other.

Lee threw another log in the fireplace, and they had ham sandwiches and beer in front of the crackling warmth of the fire, sitting Indian style on the rug.

Lee sat staring into the flames, elbows on his knees, frowning. Finally, he turned to Karen and smiled. "You're pretty special yourself, Hunter."

Impossibly thrilled, she stored away the words to remember on a cold day.

Stretching, Lee shifted position, straightening out his legs to lie on his stomach, his chin propped on his fists. "Just don't expect too much from me, nothing permanent." He glanced at her, his expression unreadable. "Freedom and space are important . . ." The last was somewhere between a statement and a question.

That wasn't what Karen had wanted to hear, and something seemed to shrivel inside of her. He had been enjoying a roll in the hay, and she had been giving her heart away. "That's fine with me," she said slowly. "Nothing heavy, no commitments." At least he wouldn't know the turmoil going on inside of her.

Lee sat up, an abrupt movement. She looked at him, surprised. His face had closed, lower lip out in a pout. If he'd had his hat on, it would have been sitting on the bridge of his nose.

"What's the matter?" she asked.

"You might have argued, or been hurt, or something."

Karen stared at him. He didn't seem to know what he wanted. "You mean you would have liked it if I'd begged. What would you have done then, spit in my eye?"

His frown melted. "Never." He reached out and took her hand. "I guess I'm a little afraid of you."

She smiled. "You ought to be; I'm really tough. You can tell by the way you get around me." After a moment, she added, "But you're right, freedom and space are important. We need to know each other much better. I do like being with you, though," she said softly, and put her arms around him.

It didn't take much time to soothe his feelings, and they made sweet love in front of the roaring fire.

By the time Lee dropped Karen off in front of her house late Sunday afternoon, she had decided to take an apartment of her own. One of the typists at the office was getting married, and hers was available immediately. Which was fortunate, because suddenly it seemed vital that Karen have the privacy of her own place. Not that she expected to spend much time alone in it.

Ten

The art show turned out to be a blessing in another way besides having brought Lee and Karen
together. Karen wrote a description of the event,
the color, the personality and elegance of the
gallery, and included many of the technical expla-
nations and descriptions that Lee and Charlie
had given. She felt it turned out well, and, with
hesitation and apprehension, took the article to
Dan Benedict. To her delight, he liked it and agreed
to run it in the next issue of the *Review*.

. After work, the typist showed Karen her apartment; she took it on the spot. The young woman
was very pleased to have the lease off her mind
and offered to move her things out within the week.

By Wednesday the apartment was empty and
ready to be cleaned and painted. After work that
day, key in hand, Karen rushed home, impatient
to look at her very own place again.

She was thrilled to see Lee's Blazer parked in front of her house. There was nothing more that she wanted than to share her excitement with him. Permanent or not, he did add a stimulus to her life.

For some reason, Lee seemed reluctant about the apartment, and Karen's spirits fell a few degrees. She had thought, had hoped, that he would like to have her alone and available in her own home.

Begrudgingly, he offered to drive her the mile and a half to see the apartment, but with much less enthusiasm than she had hoped for.

The building, a brick two-story, stood on a quiet street lined with parked cars and mature maple trees. Lee stalked after her like a disapproving shadow as she climbed the stairs to the second floor.

The apartment was small and compact, with a living room, a tiny kitchen with an attached dinette, a bedroom and a bath. It seemed deserted and friendless without furniture. The walls showed signs of hardy living and the kitchen was greasy and scummy, but the gold carpet on the floor would clean nicely, and there was a view of the mountains from the living-room window.

"It's all mine!" Karen declared happily, already painting and choosing furniture in her mind.

Lee stuck out his lower lip. "It's too small. It's not big enough to turn around in." He had his hat jammed over his eyes.

"It is for me," she disagreed stiffly. "Besides, this way there isn't as much to clean. I can think of better things to do."

"There's no counter space in the kitchen."

"I can't cook anyway."

"I saw a cockroach."

"So I'll declare war on them," she said, following him angrily, protectively.

"It's filthy. And what the hell color is that on the walls?"

"What *is* your problem?" Karen glared at him. "It can be cleaned and painted. I like it," she added defiantly.

For a few minutes, he stood silently, the expression on his face reflecting the struggle within. "Why don't you move in with me? I've got plenty of room." He looked out the window into the gathering dusk, nervously jingling the change in his pocket.

Karen stared at him, astonished. And irritated. That certainly hadn't been the most romantic proposition she'd ever heard. She walked across the room to make him face her and to push his hat back off his forehead so she could see his eyes. "What about our agreement that there'd be nothing binding?" she asked.

A lopsided grin tightened his lips. "I kind of enjoy having you around."

Now it was Karen's turn to stare out of the window. The last purple of the sunset silhouetted the mountains in the distance. They looked beautiful but so inaccessible. "I kind of like being around you too, Lee, but I need to have something of my own first, to find out who I am and what I need."

The hat jammed down over his forehead again. She reached out and took it off his head. "I need to know who you are, too. Don't do that to me; don't hide from me. Don't shut me out."

Indecision and longing warred on his face. "There's a new luxury building not far from here, the Crescent Arms. I've looked at a three-bedroom apartment there, new and clean, very nice, with a swimming pool."

"I can't afford that," she said, exasperated because he refused to understand.

"But I can. You could move in whenever you wanted."

"What are you trying to do now, Payne? Buy me? I suppose you think I'm after your money."

"I can't think of anything else to offer to convince you." He frowned heavily, as if uncomfortable without the security of his hat.

"There's always your sunny disposition," she said, exasperated. He turned away to the window. "Why can't you understand?" she said to his stiff back, then explained more gently, "If I moved into your house or apartment, they'd be just that, yours. I want something of my own for a while."

Lee turned on her aggressively, dark with anger. "If that's the way you want it, then that's the way you'll have it." His hand came up so fast, she pulled back with a frightened wince as he snatched his hat out of her hand, mashed it down on his head and stomped to the door. It slammed shudderingly after him.

"Damn you, Philip Lee Payne," she shouted at the closed door, furious with hurt. The sound of his boots clattering on the stairs faded into silence.

Walking angrily through the apartment, she raged at him because the excitement was gone, and so was he. Nothing could stop her from taking this apartment now. Nothing short of murder.

Murder? Karen glanced at the black window reflecting her image. The last trace of the sunset had disappeared. When Lee had left, the Blazer had gone with him. She was going to have to walk those dark, unfamiliar streets, alone, to get home. She swallowed nervously. He didn't even have the common decency to think about her safety. Tears dribbled down her cheeks, trickling hot and salty into the corners of her mouth. She should have expected something like this from him. After all, who was she but another woman in his long string of conquests? She walked slowly through the apartment and saw it as he had, dingy, cramped and without personality.

Dabbing at her face with the inside of the end of her jacket, she took one more tour of the place and saw it again as it could be, compact and cozy.

She had been just fine before Lee Payne had exploded in her life, and she would be again. She didn't need him! Her chin came up defiantly, settling into a stubborn line. She sighed. Liar, she said to herself.

Liar or not, she told herself as she walked through the rooms, there wasn't any hope for a future with Lee. All she could expect was disappointment and pain. She didn't need that.

Walking to the door, Karen would have given anything to have had a telephone to call a cab. But there was none, so she had no choice but to walk home through the dark streets.

Reluctantly, she turned off the light, plunging the apartment into total darkness. Feeling for the doorknob, she felt her heart speed disagreeably.

The corridor, with three other doors tightly closed against her, and the stairs leading down to the front door, were lighted with the lowest wattage the law would allow. Karen tiptoed down the steps, grimacing at each creak and rustle her feet made. When she reached the door to the outside, she cringed with fear of the unknown in the dark street. She smiled tremulously at her fear. So this was independence.

The door led out onto a porch with a railing, and there were ten steps down to the walk. Karen stood at the top, looking up and down the street. A streetlight threw a pool of light at each intersection, but in between, where the building stood, no light got by the large trees that she had admired in the light of the day. Squinting, she could barely make out cars at the curbs, and not much else.

By virtue of great courage, Karen survived her descent to the walk. In one quick glance around, she knew that each shadow had to be concealing every rapist and mugger in the city.

With ordered, marching steps, gripping the strap of her purse with a tight fist, she started toward the sidewalk.

To her horror, her worst fear materialized. She heard the sound of footsteps behind her, and then a dark shape moved out of the shadows beside the porch. The hysterical scream couldn't get past the paralysis in her throat. A hand touched her shoulder. Her eyes pinched shut, and her heart leaped like a cornered rat.

"You want a ride, lady?"

Karen threw herself into Lee's arms, almost up-ending him with the force of her shaking body. She dug her face into his shoulder. "My *God*, Payne! You scared the daylights out of me. Am I ever glad to see you. What are you *doing* lurking in dark corners terrorizing women?"

Lee held her close and safe, stroking her hair. "I didn't mean to scare you. I was just waiting for you to come out so I could apologize for making a fuss about the apartment. I like the apartment. I like you." He dropped a kiss on her hair. "I'm a stubborn idiot, and I always have to have my own way. I'm selfish and unreasonable. Does that cover everything?"

Karen nodded. Her shaking had diminished to simple trembling.

Lee kissed her hard, then gently. He pried her arms off his neck and held her hand as they walked to the Blazer. He opened the door and peered at her with a frown as she climbed in. "You thought I'd left you here with no way to get home, didn't you? What kind of a person do you think I am?"

"I didn't think any such thing," Karen said, shamefacedly. "And you didn't cover everything. You didn't offer to take me out to dinner."

When he got in the car beside her, Karen pulled his head down and kissed him back thoroughly with all the gratitude she felt that he was still here to make her whole again.

Eleven

At seven-thirty on Saturday morning, Karen stood in the middle of the living room in her empty apartment, surrounded by a pile of newspapers, an old kitchen chair, four gallons of paint, a wide paintbrush, a narrow one, and a brand-new, fuzzy paint roller. She looked up at the ceiling and felt her first misgivings. It had seemed so simple in the planning. It had to be done by Monday, when her new furniture was scheduled for delivery.

The sound of a key in the lock lifted the hairs on the back of her neck. The landlord had the only other key, but surely he would knock first. She tightened her knuckles on the big paintbrush she held and lifted it like a weapon.

The door swung open. Lee poked his head in, took one look at her and laughed. "I didn't scare you again, did I?"

"Whatever gave you that idea, Payne?" Karen let

the paintbrush drop. "And just where did you get a key?"

"I had one copied from the one you left on your dresser at your mother's house." He looked around calculatingly. "Need some help?"

"Where do you get off snooping around in my things for keys? Don't answer—I don't even know why I'm surprised. And, yes, I need help. Badly."

"What happened to all that independence?" he asked with an annoying smile. Karen raised the paintbrush, and he laughed, making for the door. When he had finished unloading the Blazer, he had added a sawhorse, a stepladder, a drop cloth, and several brushes and rollers to her meager collection. He also stocked the refrigerator with steaks and salad for dinner, and beer and sandwiches for lunch.

"Now," he said, "maybe we can get this job done and you'll have a little time to spare for me. Do you plan on furnishing this place?"

"Uh-huh," she said. "The furniture comes Monday."

"A bed?"

"Well, of course." She grinned. "I picked that out first."

"Single?"

"Uh-uh, queen."

"You'll get lost in it, all by yourself."

"Maybe I'll invite company once in a while."

"All right!" Lee said, and kissed her soundly.

"But if we don't get started with the painting," Karen said, pulling back reluctantly, "I won't be ready for the furniture on Monday."

"Then we'd better get to it, hadn't we? If we start in the bedroom, we can be sure that much is

ready." He winked, then picked up the drop cloth.
"Which can of paint?"

Karen brought the paint and pried the cover
off. It was a soft peachy pink.

"Sissy color," Lee said.

"Why not?" Karen said. "I'm a girl. I thought
you'd noticed."

He laughed and took a baseball cap out of his
back pocket to cover his hair. "Oh, I had, believe
me." He groped tantalizingly at a few sensitive
areas of Karen's body.

She pushed him away and clicked with her
tongue. "Honestly, the kind of help that's available nowadays." She poured a little paint and
started edging around a window.

"Nag, nag, nag," Lee muttered cheerfully, and
applied the first clean swath of paint on the ceiling with a roller. "What kind of furniture did you
choose?"

"Early American."

"With ruffles?" He grimaced.

"And flowers," Karen said, defensively. "Nag, nag,
nag." They both laughed.

For the rest of the day, they worked side by
side, laughing and talking, teasing and arguing,
comparing ideas and opinions. They quickly found
there wasn't a thing they didn't disagree passion-
ately about. After a short lunch break, they finished the living room in a creamy off-white. By
the time the sun went down, the apartment
sparkled, and a brisk breeze blew through the
open windows to clear the smell out.

Lee sat on the sawhorse with a can of beer, his
legs stretched out, boots crossed comfortably, looking around the room with a satisfied expression.

Karen stood behind him, pressed against his

back, her arms around his neck, hands crossed over his chest. She nuzzled the curly hairs on the back of his neck. "Thanks for the help, Payne. I'd never have gotten done without you."

He took one of her hands and kissed her palm, then tucked her hand close around him again. "It was fun, Hunter. I enjoyed it. And that's a compliment to you, in case you don't realize it. I hate painting—walls, that is."

Kissing his neck, she held him as close as she could, her body recording and awakening. She couldn't get close enough to satisfy the feeling she had, as if she'd been empty all her life and the touch of him filled the barrenness to overflowing. "Hey, Payne," she whispered against his ear.

"Hm?" he murmured.

"I love you." The words eased out softly, without thought or plan, and they felt so right on her tongue.

Absolute silence. Lee didn't actually stiffen, but his body was so motionless he didn't seem to breathe. Karen held her breath with him, waiting for him to say something, anything.

Nothing. She started to draw away, hurt, wishing she could take the words back into her mouth. She felt naked and defenseless.

Taking her hands quickly, Lee held her and didn't let her go, pulling her close to his back again. "Why, Karen?" he whispered thickly.

She breathed again. The 'why' had sounded incredulous. "I don't know," she whispered, cocking her head to look into his face. His eyes were tightly closed. "Because you're fun and funny; you make me laugh. Because you're nice to look at and nice to hold, and you make me feel all woman." She sighed and lay her head on his shoulder.

"Because your hair curls at the back of your neck. How should I know why? I just do. I just feel it. Because you're you, some good and some bad, and never, never boring."

For a long time, Lee sat silently, not moving a muscle. Then he took her hands and put them on his face. She felt the dampness on his cheeks, and it brought answering tears to her own eyes. "You can do a lot better than me, Karen." He stopped her before she could protest. "I know what you'd like to hear, but I can't say the words," he said softly, his voice husky. "They simply won't come."

"I'm not asking for anything, Lee," she whispered. "And you don't have to say the words. I know."

Pulling away, she came around in front of him and stood between his knees to put her arms around him, pulling his head down on her shoulder, laying her face on his hair. He held her so tightly it took her breath away.

Finally, Karen pulled away and took his face in her hands, looking into his eyes. She kissed him gently on the lips, then stood back and wiped her mouth. "You taste like paint, Payne." She looked at him critically. "For someone who paints for a living, you sure make a mess of yourself. You've got white measles."

The intensity in Lee's face disappeared in a puckish grin. He picked up her edging brush, still clotted with white paint, and gave her a swipe from her chin down into the V of her blouse. "I hope the shower in this place works, Hunter," he said.

"Payne, you rat!" She pulled her blouse gingerly

away from the slimy paint. "It does, but I didn't bring either towels or soap."

"I didn't think you would," Lee laughed, rummaging in one of his boxes. "Now the question is, should I be chauvinistic and let you go first, or let you be liberated and I'll go first?"

Karen took his hand and pulled him into the bathroom. "It'll hold two, won't it? Then we won't have to fight over it."

The paint-smeared clothing fell away. They stood under the spray, close together, engrossed in each other.

"You are so beautiful," Lee murmured, water flowing down around the wonder in his eyes, the bar of soap in his hand satiny against the wet curve of her neck.

She leaned her forehead against the strength of his warm shoulder for a moment, then looked up into his face. "And I've never seen anyone as marvelous as you. I feel so lucky, I can't stand it." Closing her eyes, she let her head fall back, moaning to feel the sweet smelling soap circling her breasts, circling all over her body and under. "What did I do to deserve someone like you?"

"Heaven forbid that anyone deserve me," he answered as she took the soap away from him and gave him a thorough soaping. He caught her wrist and kissed it. "What kind of a sinful life have you led, to be *given* me?"

"I'd been a saint until you came along," Karen answered and put her arms around him, pressing her water slicked body against the bulk of his, her head fitting perfectly under his chin. "You're my reward."

They stepped out of the shower and forgot the

towels; instead, they made love reverently and wetly on the freshly cleaned carpet.

They lay together in each other's arms and Karen whispered wonderingly, "I love you, Lee Payne. I really do." Then again. "I love you so much." She realized she had never felt this way before. "My feelings are as mysterious as if I were a stranger in a new land."

Very gently, Lee pushed back her tumbled, wet hair and looked into her face with dark eyes that seemed as deep as eternity. "Karen, oh, God! Karen!" He burrowed his face into her shoulder. "I need you. Please don't ever stop loving me."

She held him tightly in her arms, as if by some caprice of fate he might be taken from her.

That night, and all day Sunday, they spent in the cloistered intimacy of Lee's mountain home. Civilization didn't exist; they were alone with the trees and the hills, Lee's intense paintings and passionate body and Karen's wonder and desire. The house was a refuge from the world.

On the top of the mountain, Lee put the finishing touches on the green lady who wasn't green any longer. The portrait was radiant.

Karen looked at it. "She's beautiful. The expression on her face, it's . . . I can't explain it, but her husband is going to love the painting."

Lee put his arms around her. "I had trouble with that, but this morning when I looked at you, the expression on your face was just what I had been trying to get on hers."

"I'm not sure that I'm not jealous of her," Karen said, kissing his chin. "I don't want you touching any other women. Not even the painting of one."

"There isn't another woman in the world. Just you," he whispered. "Do you have to go home tonight? Stay. The *Review* can get along without you. I can't."

"Don't ask too much, Lee," Karen said gently. "I want to be with you, too, but I can't give up everything else."

"You said you loved me," he said, pulling away.

"I do, truly I do, Lee."

"Then stay—prove that you love me."

Something sank like lead inside Karen. She held her hand out pleadingly. "Prove . . . ? How? By giving up my being?"

Lee's hat went down over his forehead. "How do I know you care about me, if you don't want to be with me? I've got to *know* you love me."

"But I've got to know you care about *me*, too," Karen cried. "I've got needs of my own. You can't own me. You won't even say you love me."

Lee turned his back and stared at the portrait on the easel. When he turned back toward Karen, he grinned sheepishly and pushed his hat back. "Hunter, I wonder if you'll find the patience to put up with me. I've never let myself become involved with anyone before, and it frightens me."

Karen smiled with relief. "I'm scared too, Payne. You aren't the only one who's sensitive. That's why we've got to go slow and make it right."

He nodded. "Agreed. Unfortunately, I'm childish enough to want everything right now, this minute." Shooing her out of the studio, he locked the sliding doors. "I'm going to take you home now and leave you there. But I'm not happy about it," he added, smiling to let her know he was trying to understand.

Twelve

The furniture had been delivered, and Karen took Monday afternoon off to arrange and rearrange it, then move it around again, until she was moist with perspiration and felt satisfied. Humming happily, she showered, washed her hair, put on a new robe and sat down on her new davenport. The robe hadn't been a necessary item in the budget, but she hadn't been able to resist it. Its pale-yellow fleece with deep creamy ruffles of French lace at the neck and sleeves had been irresistible, and she knew the color complemented her fair coloring and hair. Besides, it looked good against the puffy davenport, with its muted gold and beige flowers. And its ruffle. She smiled and patted the shiny maple coffee table in front of her, very pleased with her gold and cream home, with its greens and browns for accent. Very satisfied with her very own home. She lifted a glass of celebratory wine and wished Lee were here.

As if her thought had materialized him, a key sounded in the lock, and Karen jumped up to welcome him with a hug and a kiss. He had to like the apartment, he simply had to.

First he admired Karen, his dark eyes showing their approval. Then, very solemnly, with his hat covering his forehead, he stalked through the apartment, frustratingly silent. Karen followed apprehensively on his heels, ready to do battle for her taste.

He inspected the sparkling kitchen, the maple dinette set, analyzed the living-room furniture, tested the cushion of a brown wing chair, then the davenport, and checked the fluffy olive-green towels in the bath. For several minutes, he stood staring at the velveteen patchwork spread on the big bed, then peered into the oversized, walk-in closet. Finally, he sat down on the bed, bounced a couple of times and frowned irritatingly.

Karen felt like hitting him. "For heaven's sake say something," she demanded. "What do you think of it?"

"Okay, Hunter, listen closely, because you'll probably never hear this again," he said solemnly. "I'm going to concede that I might have been wrong." He pushed his hat up and grinned sheepishly. "I wouldn't have given you two bits for this place when I first saw it, but you've done a great job with it. I like it. I like it very much."

Karen pushed him back on the bed and bounced on him. "You nut," she said, finding his lips and nuzzling under his chin.

"Hey, don't get carried away. I've been working all day and I'm hungry. Aren't you going to feed me?" His hands were doing delicious things to her body.

"Better settle for this, Payne. I told you I can't cook, and I'm not going to learn by experimenting on you."

"In that case, why don't you get changed into something more fitting and I'll take you out to a fancy place to eat. We'll celebrate."

Karen had her hands inside his shirt. "Why should I get dressed up, when you look like this?" His work shirt had paint stains on the front and a rip in one shoulder.

"If you can bear to let me get up, maybe I can do something about it." He rolled her off and got up.

In a few minutes, he had brought a brown velvet sport jacket, a tan turtleneck sweater and slacks from the car, along with an electric razor and various toilet articles for seeding in Karen's apartment. They had a glorious night out and finished it off with a thorough christening of the new bed.

Within a week, the seed had germinated into a full complement of masculine trappings. Deodorant and shaving lotion in her bathroom. Several of his artist's costumes crowded her closet, along with his dressy city clothes. There were at least three cameras on her shelves at all times. Karen played hostess to his clothes and, more often than not, the man himself. She was sublimely happy.

The first argument wasn't earth-shattering. It seemed silly in retrospect. It happened one evening when Karen had brought a couple of manuscripts home to read and edit.

Lee sat across from her at the dinette table watching her read, frown, mutter and make marks with her red pencil. After a while, he got up to stand behind her, reaching down to squeeze her breasts gently, kissing the side of her neck.

It was pleasant, very, but distracting. Karen brushed him off, murmuring, "In a minute . . . let me finish this." She could tell that he felt neglected, and she meant to remedy that as soon as she finished one more page.

Pulling away from her abruptly, he batted a hanging plant irritably, sending it swaying on its macrame hanger, and sulked into the kitchen, where he clattered about, straightening some of the mess of coins, papers and books on the counter.

In another few minutes, his angry rattling distracted Karen. She looked up. "What are you doing?" she demanded.

All the dishes and cookware were heaped on the counter alongside the canned goods and staples. He gave her a disgusted look. "I'm organizing your cupboards. As far as I can tell, you've jammed everything in without any kind of plan." He stood hipshot, defying her to disagree.

He was right; she had jammed them in. It made her fiercely angry to be confronted with the fact. "I had it just the way I wanted it. You put everything back where you found it," she ordered. "If you want to organize a kitchen, go organize your own, Lee Payne. This is mine."

For one thunderously silent second, Lee glared at Karen. Then he smashed his hat down over his eyes and stomped to the door. "If that's the way you want it, then, damn it, I will. You're as much fun as a zombie, with your nose buried in papers all the time." The door shuddered in its frame after him.

"That's fine!" she yelled after him. "That's just fine. Maybe I can get something done now."

The manuscript shook in her hands as she made herself read. The words wouldn't register, even after she'd read the same sentence five times. "Why can't he understand?" she asked the empty room.

Empty room. Too empty. If she hurried, perhaps she could catch him. "Lee," she called, running to the door to yank it open. He stood just outside, with his fist raised to knock. Karen bowled him over with her hug.

The next quarrel was much more personal and wounding. After a week, the October issue of the *Review* had been completed and was out. Karen's article about the opening of the art show had been printed under her very own name. She was ecstatic, and Lee celebrated with her, taking her proudly to a fantastic dinner at the Brown Palace in downtown Denver.

With the October issue out, the office went into its early-month slow-down. Karen enthusiastically resumed working on Lee's personality sketch. She knew exactly how she wanted to present him, as an exciting, brilliant artist from an underprivileged background that he had overcome with courage and strength of character.

He wasn't pleased. "You've already been published," he protested, "why do you need this now? I don't want to be written about. I've never wanted to be written about. My life is private. Nobody needs to know anything about me. They can look at my paintings or my photos and know all they need to."

Karen didn't understand. "It's not as if you're a hermit or a recluse, or even a terribly private person. You're always in the limelight somewhere. What's the difference if the limelight happens to be words printed on paper?"

He crossed his arms stubbornly across his chest, standing over her belligerently. "If you can write an article about my work, describing and explaining it, fine, but leave my life out of it."

"Everyone knows about your work; that's been written about dozens of times." Karen stood in her living room, holding out several typewritten papers. "Won't you just read it? Maybe you won't hate it as much as you think. I'm not doing a hatchet job, you know."

Turning away, he growled, "I don't want to read it. I won't read it."

"Lee—" Karen put the papers on the coffee table and reached out to touch his arm, "even though I've had that one little piece published in the *Review*, that's not enough to catch anyone's attention. I need something important that I can use as a lever to get a position with more opportunity." She tried to turn him to face her, make him look at her. He pulled away and went to the window, offering her a view of his stiff back.

"Big deal," he said. "Now I'm a lever. Is that all I mean to you?"

His attitude angered her. "That's not true, and you know it. I care about you, but this is important too."

"No, I don't know it." He turned abruptly and glared at her. "I don't know why I'm arguing about this. I can think of a dozen other women who would be glad to do anything to make me happy and have my company."

Jealousy added itself to her anger and reddened Karen's face. "I'm sure you can. Chastity for one, I suppose."

"Yes," Lee said, smiling a nasty little smile. "Chastity for one. She'd drop anything for me."

"Well, who the hell is stopping you?" Karen screamed.

The door slammed with a crash that knocked a bauble off a shelf, which chased itself around in circles on the floor. Karen kicked it and listened to it shatter against the wall. Tears flooded down her cheeks.

It took ten full minutes for her to calm down, to put the image of Lee with Chastity out of her mind. And she herself had sent him right into that hateful woman's arms. She beat her head with her fists. "You idiot. You idiot!" she whispered.

Looking at the door, she knew he had left too long ago to catch. But maybe, just maybe . . . She tore to the door and dashed out into the hall to fall with a resounding crash over Lee's legs. He sat on the floor just outside her door, legs stretched out. Jumping up, he picked Karen up, checking her over for broken bones, murmuring apologetically.

Except for grazed knees and elbows, Karen found herself to be whole and uninjured. She felt perversely disappointed that nothing had been chipped but her pride. "You're always lurking around, Payne." Then the ludicrousness of the accident hit her, and she laughed.

Lee smiled. "I wasn't lurking, Hunter. I was waiting. I knew you'd come running after me," he said complacently.

Karen hated to be reminded that she was so

predictable, but the spectre of Chastity's availability kept her from taking him to task.

His bright, engaging smile melted her resentment as Lee put his arm around her to help her back into the apartment. "I'm sorry I'm acting like a spoiled kid again." He enveloped her in his arms, and she snuggled her face into his shoulder with a sigh.

"I, ah . . ." Lee started, then stopped. Karen looked up at him. "Go ahead and do that stupid article. I suppose it won't kill me."

Two days later, while they were lying in bed in the cozy afterglow of lovemaking, Lee asked Karen if she wanted to go to Santa Fe with him on Thursday. After he took care of some business, they could sightsee and visit Charlie Whitehorse.

There was nothing Karen would rather have done, but it would mean taking off at least two working days. She couldn't imagine suggesting time off to Dan Benedict. She needed her job, especially now that she had the apartment.

After hesitating and pondering, she finally said, "I really wish I could go. I loved Charlie, and I'd give anything to meet his wife and children, but I can't take the time off."

"Oh, damn," Lee said pulling away from her and turning on his side with his back to her face. "I don't know why I bothered asking."

Karen massaged his shoulders placatingly. "Don't be angry. If you aren't doing anything Sunday, I'd love to spend the day with you in the mountains at your place."

"I'm going to be busy. I've got to bring my

canvases and materials down off the hill before winter sets in."

"Oh, come on, don't be pouty. I can help you." She slipped her hands under the sheet and found a few spots that made him shiver with pleasure.

He caught her hand, directed its placement to suit himself and turned back to her with a smile. "A fine help you are. You won't even let me stay mad at you." His arms went around her, his face into her tumbled hair. "Sunday, then. I'll accept the crumbs you drop for me."

The aspens were in full color, pouring brilliant mustard-yellow down the mountainsides. The ground cover had turned vibrant crimson and the air smelled as crisp and heady as hard cider. Chipmunks and ground squirrels ran like Furies to find and store the last seeds. Karen and Lee stood on the rim of the hill, enthralled by the beauty around them.

She looked down the steep trail they had climbed. "Aren't you afraid you'll ruin your canvases, dragging them down there?"

Lee grinned. "I wouldn't think of risking them; I've put too much effort into them." He took her hand to lead her to the side of the hill. There, hidden from view by boulders and brush, was an easy, neat set of railroad-tie stairs.

Karen stared in amazement. "Do you mean to say that you've been forcing me to crawl up that cliff, when these have been here all the time?"

"The exercise did you good, didn't it? Besides, I like the view when I'm climbing up behind you."

One of the dogs, Freak, pushed against her, licking her hand in a bid for attention. She fondled the thick fur. When she straightened, she smiled at Lee. "I hate to think of this summer coming to an end. It's been fun."

Lee gave her a long, intense look, as if analyzing her words. "You sound like everything is in the past tense."

"Summer *is* in the past tense. It's over, and I've loved it." Looking around, she felt a comfort and warmth on Lee's mountaintop that she'd never known before, and sighed. "I never dreamed anything like this would happen when I first walked into your studio last August." She smiled. "I thought you were a displaced ranch hand when I first saw you, did you know that?"

Lee walked into the small house to stand in front of an embryonic painting on an easel. Its subject was a pair of figures, male and female, just emerging from colors that were softer and more gentle than usual.

When he turned back toward her, there was a defensive edge in his voice. "And you looked like a little girl all dressed up in your mother's clothes, but despite that, you got what you wanted, didn't you? An interview with P. Lee Payne. An in-depth interview." He sat down in the chair to rock back on its legs.

Unsure of the intent behind his words, Karen moved close to put her hands on his shoulders. "The article will come out in the next issue of the *Review*. So that's over—we can forget it," she said, hoping to reassure him.

The front legs of the chair came down with a thump. "Oh, Lord! That's it, then." He got up and ripped a page off a pad of paper on the table. "But you forgot one thing," he said bitterly, writing with an angry scrawl in marking pencil. "I'll even

give you written permission to publish that gar-
bage." He stuffed the slip of paper in the pocket of
her blouse. "Now summer is officially over. You've
got everything you started out to achieve. You can
give me your 'so long, it's been nice knowing you,
and thanks a lot' speech, confident that your article is safe and legal. Right, Karen Jane?" he said,
his words rich with sarcasm.

"Lee, will you listen?" she said, suddenly realizing that he'd thought she meant their affair was
over when she said summer was over. "I didn't
mean—"

"Didn't mean what?" he interrupted. "Didn't
mean to let your enterprise get out of hand?" His
face was angry and hurt under his hat. "I've
watched it coming. You could say 'I love you' easily enough, but you always qualified it with 'Don't
get too close.' " He picked up the canvas from the
easel, his fists tight on its wooden frame. "You've
been using me to get what you want with all the
finesse of a born sneak, with your 'old friend'
routine and your convenient empty gas tank."

"Lee, you're wrong," she cried, hurt and angry
because he wouldn't listen or try to understand.
"It isn't like that. I do love you. I don't want you to
think this of me. It isn't true."

"You wouldn't know the truth if it hit you in the
eye, Karen Jane." His voice rasped like chalk on a
blackboard, his fists clenching and unclenching
on the frame of the picture. "It's been an interesting and educational experience. I've learned something from it too. I've learned to trust my own
intuition, and that tells me to never trust anyone
who comes bearing the gift of love."

Tears stung Karen's eyes. "What gives you the
right to act so superior? You aren't open or hon-

est yourself. At least I know how to give love, and I'd know how to accept it, if anyone offered it to me. You can't even *say* the words I love you," she said. Tears dribbled down her cheeks, and it angered her to lose control. "Philip Lee," she tacked on sarcastically, mimicking his derisive use of "Karen Jane."

The dark fury on his face turned her knees to water. She would have given anything in the world to be able to take that "Philip" back.

The canvas and frame were lifted high. Karen cringed, as they came down with a shattering crash against the wall, collapsing into a broken heap of ripped cloth and splintered wood.

Karen rushed down the steps she had never used, urged on in the face of Lee's silent wrath. An icy heaviness in her chest told her that this was irrevocably the end.

The ride down out of the mountains was so fast that Karen shrank down into the seat of the Blazer, too frightened to look out of the car window.

She might have made an attempt to reason with Lee when they neared the city. But even that was made impossible when, five miles from home, a siren and flashing red lights signaled that Lee's speed had caught the attention of the highway patrol. Karen dared not look at him the rest of the way, as he drove, infuriated, at fifty-five, with his ticket on the dashboard.

Within half an hour of their arrival, Lee had systematically removed every trace of himself from her apartment, while Karen stood by helplessly watching.

The last thing he did was thump his key to her apartment down on the coffee table with a metallic click. Then, without a word, Lee Payne walked out of her door and out of her life.

She hadn't even had a kiss to remember him by this time. Karen threw herself on the bed that was much too big for one person, to weep tears that were acid and bitter. They didn't help; they didn't begin to relieve her pain.

Thirteen

By the middle of October, Karen began to enter the world of the living again. In the days since Lee had left her, she had walked around in a mechanical stupor, taking care of those things that had to be done in a haze of abstraction.

One morning, she took a few minutes to open the folder holding the article she had written about Lee, laying the pictures and pages out on her desk. She hated every scrap of paper, every word. If she had never written it, the break between them wouldn't have occurred.

A rap at her door interrupted her thoughts. Dan Benedict came in. Standing in front of her desk, he looked down at the article. "Is this what you did on P. Lee Payne?"

Karen nodded silently.

With a grunt, Dan sat on the edge of her desk to pick up the typewritten pages. He read them, then

looked at the pictures, examples of Lee's oil paintings and photo art. He cleared his throat. "You've
done a good job."

"Thanks," Karen answered bitterly.

Dan looked at her, frowning. "Should we run it
in the November issue?"

She shook her head. "No. I don't think so."

Nodding, Dan carefully straightened the pages
and put them down. "The *Denver Post* would take
it, I'm sure."

Karen leaned back in her chair and rocked
slowly. "I don't know what I'm going to do with
it." She watched Dan apprehensively. It was apparent he had more on his mind than a few
minutes' of idle conversation.

He heaved his hip off of her desk and ambled to
the door. "You'd better think about offering the
article on Payne to someone," he said, "because
the reason I came in here was to tell you that the
owners of the *Review* have decided that it's been
a money-losing proposition for too long. They're
putting it to bed, permanently."

Karen stood up, gripping the edge of her desk.
"Oh, no! You mean they're giving it up? When?"

"This will be our last issue, the one we're working on now. So as soon as we get everything
straightened out and sold, we'll be looking for
new jobs. The Payne article might be the pawn
you need to go on to bigger and better things. It's
good, you know, and it's salable." He put a hand
on the doorknob and frowned back at her. "So
use it. What have you got to lose?" he urged, and
went out.

Idly fingering the folder on Lee, Karen stared at
it blindly. Should she use it? Nothing could make
him more angry or hate her any worse than he

did already. She toyed with the folder. It was probably the only bit of bargaining power she had.

"I can see by the mournful look on your face that you've had the bad news dropped on you," Hank Mitchell said, startling her. She hadn't heard him come in. He sat on the edge of her desk and took a deep breath, which he let out explosively. "What are you going to do now?"

Karen leaned back in her chair. "I don't know—look around and see if there's another job available before you get to it, I guess." She smiled bleakly. "What about you?"

He shrugged. "I thought maybe I'd marry a rich wife."

"Well, don't look at me, I can't help you out there."

"Too bad. How about you marrying a rich husband and keeping me on the side? How about Payne, the urban cowboy?"

She made a face. "No luck there either. That's all over. Passé."

"Then we're going to have to pound the pavement." He leaned his elbow on his knee and his chin on his fist. "Maybe I'll write a book and make a million bucks."

"What about?"

"A couple of people, a beautiful woman and a handsome, talented man, who, when they lose their jobs, collaborate on a book, only to starve to death before it's finished."

Karen laughed. "Oh, it's going to be a documentary. I thought you were talking about fiction."

Hank smiled. "If your Payne episode is really over, maybe you'd consider going out with me tonight. We can drown our sorrows with beer and pizza. That's all I can afford, but it's Friday night and there'll be crowds of happy people around, and some of their enthusiasm might rub off on us."

"I'd like that," Karen answered, and meant it. She'd had enough of hashing over what might have been and worrying about the future. "We'll go Dutch, though; I don't want you starving at the end before I do."

Later that evening, Karen slipped into a full, gathered skirt of a rich shade of blue and a full, long-sleeved Slavic peasant blouse with embroidery around a slit neckline. As she pulled on a pair of snug black boots, she found she was pleased about going out with Hank. She had thought she'd never enjoy anything again, but she was looking forward to tonight.

Hank picked her up at seven to take her to a dimly lit, noisy rathskeller, with red-checked tablecloths and smoky candles. They ate pizza with everything on it and drank a pitcher of dark beer. Hank had thought of no end of unlikely and imaginative possibilities for his future. Karen laughed and fantasized along with him.

At nine, a combo took the stand. The drums, trombone, bass viola and piano played old, mellow dance music: waltzes, two steps, even polkas. A good-sized dance floor attracted a crowd of couples wrapped around each other, moving and swaying to the music.

Karen looked around the smoky room, wondering what sort of people had brought ballroom dancing back. There were a number of older people, but also younger ones. Many of the men were in Denver western attire, and the women were just as casual. Everyone seemed to be enjoying themselves, laughing and talking over the noise of the music.

Karen stiffened as she watched a group enter the door, to stand just inside, looking around. There were three young women, quite beautiful, in designer jeans and silky blouses. They were accompanied by a couple of men; one of them was Lee. Oddly, with so many others in the room affecting a western look, he had on a bulky white turtleneck sweater over close-fitting slacks. Without his hat, he looked unbearably handsome, with his black hair and eyes, standing under the yellow light over the entrance.

Karen looked away quickly and turned her chair to put her back to him. Why did he have to show up here, tonight, when she hadn't thought about him, not once, for at least two hours?

"Would you like to make a stab at it?" Hank asked.

"What?"

"Dancing. Would you like to dance? It looks like fun. I've been watching, and I think I can handle it, if you're game."

Hesitating, then agreeing, Karen got up. She'd be damned if she was going to hide in her chair just because Lee happened to be here. The dancing did look like fun.

As the evening wore on, they had another pitcher of beer and danced with a little more flair, swooping and whirling within the limitations of the crowded floor. Karen felt flushed and relaxed, almost able to forget that Lee was there, at a table in the back of the room.

Able to forget, until, during a polka, another body hit hers in a jarring collision. She tripped and would have fallen but for a hand on her arm. She looked up into Lee's face. It was grim and unfriendly, his smoldering eyes on hers.

"Sorry," he said tightly, and gave her a brief, unfriendly smile.

Chastity had her body cuddled against his, and she smiled brightly at Karen, triumphantly. "So nice to see you again, darling," she murmured, and maneuvered Lee away.

Hank drew Karen back into his arms, but she had lost her sense of rhythm and asked to sit down.

Even at the table, she couldn't recapture her feeling of enjoyment. She tried, but couldn't, respond to Hank's attempts to distract her. Finally, she pleaded a headache and asked him to take her home.

At her door, Hank kissed her lightly on the lips and tapped her nose with a forefinger. "Let me know when you're really over that miserable cowboy. Okay?"

After he had left, Karen lay in her bed and cried herself to sleep.

At the end of the next week, the last edition of the *Review* had been finished and sent to the printer. There was nothing left for Karen to do but sort through her files, return the unused manuscripts and tie up loose ends. When that was done, she brought a box into her office to empty her desk.

The last things she put in the box were the article on Lee Payne and her crystal paperweight. She stood looking down at them, depressed and apprehensive now that the moment had come to leave her office and the *Review* for the last time.

She knew she could never bring herself to use the article on Lee for her personal benefit. And suddenly it seemed terribly important that he be assured that she wouldn't publish it. His privacy was so very precious to him, and he was so very precious to her.

It seemed impossible, now, that she could ever have thought one simple little article might bring her the stature her father had enjoyed. What a fool she had been to alienate Lee because of such an impossible goal.

She knew she could never bring Lee back to her, but she could give him the gift of privacy.

But how could she get it to him? Mail it? That seemed cold. Bring it to his photography studio? She couldn't face his sophisticated receptionist. Nita? She couldn't face her either, not after what she had done to Lee. She made her decision to take it to his house, hand it to him, say, "I'm sorry," and leave. What happened after that would be up to him.

Relieved by her decision, Karen picked up her box, took one final look around her empty office and walked out to say her last painful good-byes to the staff of the *Review*.

It was after six-thirty that evening when Karen started her drive to Lee's mountain house.

Beyond Evergreen, she stared at the road, her brow knitted, watching for the turnoff. Nothing seemed as familiar as it had when Lee had been driving.

And by the time she turned off on the side road,

the sun had vanished and the light had disappeared abruptly, as it does in the mountains, with no leisurely easing from day into night.

Finally, she turned into Lee's driveway, but then the fence barred her way and she muttered a few choice words, debating what to do. Perhaps it was unlocked. She climbed out of the car and walked to the gate to finger the solid padlock and jerk at it in frustration.

Cupping her hands around her eyes to shield them from the glare of the headlights, Karen sat and thought, trying to come up with a place to leave the folder. There was no mailbox; Lee got his mail at the studio in Denver. The wind would take it if she left it in the open. Under a rock? He might not see it.

Reaching for the gearshift, Karen backed the car down the driveway. The headlights flashed on a pine tree beside the locked gate. Karen braked quickly.

Staring at the tree thoughtfully, she remembered Lee climbing it to get his spare key when she had hidden his. She debated whether she could climb it, then shook her head. The lower branches were too high. Unless . . . She put the car in first and inched close, then shut the motor off and took a penlight out of the glove compartment.

Standing on the fender of the car, Karen reached up and grasped the rough bark of the branch. It smelled strongly of pine and left sticky pitch stains on her hands. She knew she'd ruin a good pants suit, but it didn't seem to matter.

Making her way cautiously from branch to branch, inch by inch, with one eye on the black pit below, her tiny light stabbing the darkness like a needle, she searched. Just as she decided it was hopeless, she found it, a small metal box wired to the tree trunk. Inside was a ring with three keys. Bless Lee for being so organized. Putting the key ring in her pocket, she reached down with one foot and began her descent. Painfully, slowly, she felt her way down through the stabbing pine needles, picking each handhold with the utmost care, gasping each time the wind caught the tree to make it sway nauseatingly. One more branch to go, then the fender.

When she had hopped safely back on the ground, Karen took the folder out of the box in the car and, as an afterthought, the crystal paperweight.

The padlock opened with no trouble, and Karen walked up the drive to the house. The dogs barked viciously as she stepped on the porch, and her feet faltered. She hadn't thought about them. Would they know her well enough to let her in?

Slipping the key into the lock on the front door, she turned it, then wavered as the barking on the other side of the door crescendoed. She hadn't climbed that tree to be stopped by a pair of mutts. Nor had she survived to be chewed into hamburger.

Finally, with her heart in her throat, she turned the key, then the knob, and cracked the door open to peek in. The two German Shepherds put their shoulders to the door and pushed it open, forcing Karen back. Both sets of teeth were white and menacing, the fur standing up straight on their shoulders in the darkness.

"Freak? Sally?" Karen pleaded, her voice hollow, her pulse thundering. Both stiff bodies relaxed into wriggling happiness. She nearly fell flat under the onslaught of tongues and paws. "Down,

down," she called weakly, and walked into Lee's house with a dog at each side.

Feeling carefully along the dark wall with her pitch-sticky hand, Karen found the light switch and lit the house. It waited for her, silent and empty as a tomb, its memories pressing in around her so painfully that she moaned. Freak nudged her with her nose and looked up at her with limpid brown eyes.

Karen walked into the living room to stand beside the dead fireplace, with its residue of ash from yesterday's welcoming fires. The beams hung overhead, seeming to press her down. The children in the picture stared dolefully, accusingly, out at her. She turned her eyes quickly away from them, and moaned again. The ghost of Lee was here, everywhere, all around her, watching, waiting, accusing.

Very slowly, with a dog on either side, she walked through the house, torturing herself with its familiarity. The kitchen, all the rooms, were open, including one that she hadn't seen—Lee's studio. All of his paintings had been brought down from the mountaintop. They were stacked in untidy piles along the walls. No new paintings had been started. Instead, the photo that had been displayed at the gallery rested on an easel in the middle of the room. The rest hung on the walls, four others, each done with loving care, showing her laughing, angry, pensive, sad. Karen looked at them for a long time and wondered why he hadn't destroyed them. A kernel of hope tried to sprout in her heart, but she knew it was useless. He'd never let her get close enough to hurt him again. She turned and left the studio.

With painful, dragging steps, Karen walked up

the stairs to the bedroom beyond the balcony, the two dogs pressing close. She wondered whether they were monitoring her or whether they were lonely and feeling neglected. She knelt for a moment to put her arms around each one.

Lee's bedroom tore viciously at the wound in her heart. She sniffled and smeared pine pitch on her cheeks as she wiped away her tears. Every part of the room seemed so much a part of herself, the polished chests, the burlap on the walls, a chair she'd seen Lee sit in to pull on his boots. The heavy, rust-colored bedspread, the pillow her head had rested on, and his.

Being in the room itself was torture enough, but the clothes that had been tossed hastily on the bed were too much to bear. Karen touched his jeans, the shape of him still rounding them, then felt his work shirt. When she hugged it to her face, it smelled of Lee, a musky, sweet, precious smell. She touched his hat, tracing the brim with her finger, stroking the felt. Then she wondered where he had gone after he had changed, and could stand it no longer. She put the folder down on the bed beside his hat and, after a brief hesitation, lay the crystal paperweight on top of it.

Hastily, Karen made her way to the door. She stuck the key in the keyhole on the inside and left it hanging. Then she went out, shut the door securely, hurried down the drive, closed the gate, fastened the padlock and climbed into her car, to drive desolately down off his mountain.

Fourteen

Almost two weeks after Karen had started hunting for a job, she accepted the fact that nothing was available in the journalistic field.

She got up early that morning and looked through the want ads of the *Denver Post* one more time. She had already pored over them last night and circled the secretarial positions that she might try, but they were meager and seemed uninteresting.

Furnishing the apartment had almost wiped out her savings, and it was imperative that she find work soon, any kind of work. Her spirits had dropped from low to panicky.

Pouring a cup of freshly perked coffee, she sat down at the table in her robe and looked at the circled ads. She chewed her pencil and sipped from her cup, then decided to go to the employment agency early to check for secretarial situations.

Dispirited, she showered and shampooed her hair, then dressed carefully in a soft white blouse and a dark-green corduroy suit that looked professional but not severe, and pulled on a pair of brown boots. She didn't think she looked like a little girl dressed up in her mother's clothes, as Lee had put it. Lee. Forget Lee. How?

At eight-thirty she had another fifteen minutes before she had to leave to arrive at the agency at nine. Draping her jacket carefully over a dinette chair, she sat down with a fresh cup of coffee. Her only hope was to fill out applications and pray.

A knock on the door startled her. Damn, she thought. It was probably the landlord. He had been pressuring her to either sign a new lease for an additional six months or agree to vacate the apartment. She was in no mood for a confrontation with him today. She had two more weeks before she had to give notice, and he could just wait.

Angrily, Karen marched to the door to jerk it open as the knock was repeated, her face set and angry. The anger turned to surprise. Her heart rebounded alarmingly around her rib cage.

Lee stood in the hallway outside her door, smartly dressed in a beautifully fitted tan tweed sport coat and sparkling white shirt, and he even wore a tie. Dark-brown polished shoes had replaced his cowboy boots, and his hat was nowhere in evidence. His presence and his urban appearance mystified her. Her hand went unconsciously to her breast, protecting the hurt there. His face gave no hint of his intention; he neither smiled nor frowned, just stood there, waiting.

"May I come in?" he asked, quite formally, his deep voice low.

"Oh. Yes," Karen answered, finally finding her voice. "I suppose, if you like."

"I like," he said, and walked into the living room as she stood aside. He waited there, his manner subdued and polite. She had forgotten how big he was; he seemed to overwhelm her small room.

Silently, he waited for her to take the lead, and she didn't know what to do with him, or how to behave with him; he seemed a complete stranger.

When the silence became unbearable, Karen said, "I'm having a cup of coffee. Do you want one?"

"That would be nice." He followed her into the dinette and took a seat at the table, very controlled, very proper.

Karen took down a cup and saucer, pouring coffee with hands that shook like aspen leaves. What in the devil did he want? She put the cup in front of him and took her seat across from him. She turned the circled want ads over, out of view.

"I've got an appointment, so I'll have to leave in a few minutes," she said. It was not technically an appointment, but she knew that if she sat this close to him for much longer, she was going to cry, and she couldn't bear that. That was probably what he wanted, to twist the knife in her wound, to gloat over her misery.

He nodded, acknowledging her words. "Reading the paper, are you?" he asked, his eyes on the *Post* in front of her.

"Bits and pieces," she answered. Actually, she had only looked at the help-wanted section.

Lee sipped his coffee, and Karen noticed that he had lines across his forehead that he hadn't had before, and no sparkle or mischief in his dark eyes. She knew the experience had been painful for him too, so what was he doing here, prolonging the agony? He didn't seem bent on remedying the situation. No pleas, no apologies, just idle small talk. If he thought they could be friends, he was out of his mind.

"Bits and pieces," he repeated. "You ought to read the paper thoroughly; it sharpens your mind and keeps you abreast of world affairs."

Karen shifted restlessly in her chair. "I've really got to leave in a minute, Lee. . . ."

"So do I. I've got to see a man about a duplex," he said, fingering his cup, turning it in its saucer. "You really ought to read the paper, though."

"What *is* this with the paper?" She turned the bulky newspaper and pulled off the front section. "Murders, robberies and kidnappings. I can do without that," she said. "What's this about a duplex? Are you going into real estate now?" Then, annoyed with herself, she wished she hadn't asked. She had no intention of encouraging him.

Her irritation seemed to put him at ease. He pushed back his chair slightly to cross one ankle over the other knee. The pull of his neatly fitted slacks around his thighs pained her even more. After a moment, he said carelessly, "I'm going to put the mountain house up for sale."

She stared at him, dismayed. "The house? You're selling—" She clamped her mouth shut. It was nothing to her, but she felt a thud of disappointment deep inside. She loved that house, that mountain.

"It's time I got rid of it," he explained. "The house is too isolated. It makes a good hideaway, a place to escape from the real world. Maybe it's time I joined society. Besides, it costs a fortune to heat in the winter."

There were a million questions and arguments she could have thrown at him, but she stifled them. "What do you want, Lee? I've really got to leave."

Reaching out for the paper, he unfolded it and put the Living and Arts section in front of her. "I want to be sure you read all of your damned paper."

Karen stared at him. The Living and Arts section? Society news. Marriages and engagements. That would be a reason for selling the house. A woman like Chastity would never agree to live in the middle of a woods. Surely he wouldn't be so cruel as to want to watch her read his engagement notice. She turned to the inside of that section, then turned another page and let out her breath. There was no announcement of his engagement in that column.

"Hunter! Do you have to be so dense? The first page. Will you look at the first page?" He clapped a hand down on the paper to make her look.

The spark was back in his eyes, and she knew he had guessed what she'd been looking for. Then she looked down at the page in front of her. Her hand went to her mouth to cover the gasp. Her article about Lee commanded the entire first page. Her name, as clear and thrilling as a shooting star, was printed right under the title. The pictures she had chosen illustrated his abilities, and another picture, one taken of him by a staff photographer, smiled out at her as if he'd played an enormous joke.

The words she had written were there, every one; nothing had been changed or edited. She read the article numbly, then reread it, unbelievingly, before she looked up at Lee. "You gave them the article? Why did you do it? I don't understand you."

"I don't understand me either." He uncrossed his legs and leaned forward to rest his elbows on the table and look at her sharply. "Why did you leave the article at my house? Why didn't you use it yourself?"

"I guess I didn't want you to think I was the kind of person who would do something that you hated. I didn't realize how strongly you felt about it until . . . that last day. You didn't give me a chance to say anything."

He gave a deep sigh and looked down at his cup. "At least you found out what kind of a fellow you were fooling around with before it was too late. I gave it to the *Post* as a sort of retribution." His eyes lifted, and he searched her face for a moment. She didn't respond, didn't know how to respond.

"If I'd read the thing when you asked me to," he said, "I'd never have raised such a fuss. You make me sound like some sort of courageous character out of a Horatio Alger book. Squalor to success by dint of hard work and perseverance." He tilted the cup and watched the coffee swirl. "You almost had me thankful for a life that gave me the background to develop my sensitivities into creative genius." He glanced up and twisted his lips into a wry smile. "There was nothing offensive in what you wrote, only admiration and respect, and it's forced me to take a good look at myself and my reactions to people and to situations."

Leaning back, he put his hands in his jacket pockets and raised his eyebrows. "How did you get into my place to leave the article? I thought I had a fortress."

Karen smiled slightly. "Nothing to it, for a sneak."

He winced. "I guess I had that coming. Can I take them back, all those words?"

"They're yours, I don't have to give them back. What you do with your words is your business."

His brows came down in a puzzled frown, but he didn't continue. Instead, he brought one hand out of his pocket to hold up her father's crystal paperweight. "I can understand why you gave me the article, but why this? I know how much it meant to you."

Karen looked at the sparkling glass in his hand. "I've done some soul searching of my own. It was much easier to give up my mother, she was there to shove me out of the nest, late as it was. But to come to terms with my father was quite a different thing. I suppose it was as if I had become frozen into the level of feelings I had for him as a six year old. He was a hero to me. If he had been there as I grew up, perhaps I would have come to see him as the ordinary human being he must have been. Maybe I felt responsible for the accident that killed him."

Smiling slightly, she glanced at him. "I think I gave it to you as a symbol that now I'm going to be me, that I'm not going to try to be my father's alter ego. The desperation to succeed is gone."

He put it on the table between them. "Do you still want me to have it? Are you sure you don't want it back?"

"No," Karen whispered, shaking her head. "It's valuable you know, probably not in a monetary sense, but it is valuable all the same. And I want you to have it."

He studied her face without the hint of a smile.

"Why didn't you bash me over the head with something when I said all those awful things to you?"

Karen got up quickly and carried her cup to the sink. "Don't, Lee." She rinsed the cup and wiped it with a tea towel. And wiped it. And wiped it. "There would always be something for us to fight about. There isn't any point in rehashing this. What's done is done. I'm no angel; I had just as much to do with our fight as you did. I'm selfish and stubborn too. Let's just let it be." It was almost more than she could do, to say those words. Her every instinct demanded that she go to Lee, hold him, beg him to take her, to let everything be as it had been before. But unless there was openness and honesty between them, it would only mean asking for another misunderstanding, for more quarrels.

When she realized she was still wiping the cup, she set it down on the counter with an angry thump.

"You said you had an appointment," he said. "I suppose I'd better leave so you can go to it."

Karen looked at him. He sat hunched forward, playing with the crystal paperweight, intent on it. She hesitated and thought for a moment. Honesty. "I don't have an appointment. I meant to go to an employment agency. I'm out of a job. The *Review* folded."

"I know." Lee looked up briefly, then returned his attention to the paperweight in his fingers. "Naturally I called Dan Benedict before I offered the article to the *Post*. Do you have anything lined up?"

Karen frowned. "Not yet."

He held the crystal up toward the window, watching the sparkle as the sun hit it, scattering rainbows with a slow movement of his hand. "If you call the editor of the *Post*, he said he'd be interested in talking to you about possible employment. He's impressed with the way you handled the piece."

With trembling hands, Karen filled the cup she had just polished and sat down across from him. She could hardly absorb what he had said.

He glanced at her. "If you're worried that I've used my influence to get you a job, then stop, because it would be flunky work, starting at the bottom. From there you're on your own. You'll have to sink or swim on your own."

"I'm not worried about that; I'd have used anyone's influence to get that kind of a chance. I can't believe it's happening."

Lee smiled slightly. "You could have given them the article yourself and gotten your chance."

She shook her head. "I couldn't have." She watched him for a second. "I can't believe you've done this for me. I want you to know that I appreciate it very much. I know it wasn't easy for you."

He spun the paperweight on the table, his eyes on it. "I've been doing a lot of thinking since we've been apart." The worry lines creased his forehead, and he didn't go on. Some sort of a struggle seemed to be going on inside of him.

Karen waited, then asked, "What about?"

"I suppose I was jealous of the time and interest you gave to your work, but I've realized that a lot of your attraction for me stemmed from your interests and your ambition." He glanced up. "I don't have much respect for shallow people. I'd get bored awfully fast if you didn't have something that kept you vital." Beads of perspiration were shining above his upper lip. "I've been calling myself every name in the book for being such a fool."

A lump rose in Karen's throat. She couldn't speak.

Lee looked at her miserably. "I had hoped we might be together again."

Her eyes stung. "How long do you think it would be before we fought again? I can't stand that, Lee. It's too painful. I can't bear for you to walk out on me every time we disagree."

The glass paperweight spun under his fingers as he looked down at it. "That's one of the things that I've thought about. Would it help if I say I'll try to change my ways? I can't promise anything."

She nodded. "We're too much alike, aren't we? I've got a pretty good temper of my own that I have to control. I don't know if we can do it by just wanting to."

His hand clamped down on the paperweight. "It's just that I'm so miserable away from you. I thought I couldn't stand it when I saw you dancing with that . . . person at the rathskeller."

"I know," Karen said bitterly. "I hated Chastity, too. I want to be with you, but I'm afraid. I've got to be sure of you."

Lee got slowly to his feet and walked around the table. He took her hands and pulled her up. His face was pale, and the perspiration had spread to his forehead.

Karen looked up at him. He looked ill. "Are you all right?" she asked. He held her hands so tightly, pulling them close to his chest, that it was painful. She could feel his heart racing. "Lee?" she said quickly, worried.

Minutes dragged by as he struggled with himself. Finally he took a deep breath and said quickly, "Karen, I love you more than life itself." Another breath. "If I've killed the affection you have for me with my stupidity, I might as well be dead." Another, slower breath, as if he felt relieved. "I love you, and I want you with me for the rest of my life." A bead of perspiration rolled down his cheek, and a look of sheer terror crossed his face, to be quickly controlled.

Karen pulled her hands away from his and took his face between her palms. "Oh, my darling," she whispered. "Oh, my darling, I love you too. And there is nowhere in the world that I'd rather be than with you." Her last doubt evaporating, she threw her arms around his neck and kissed his lips.

Lee's arms went around her with such intensity that she thought her ribs might crack, but she didn't care. Their lips moved together, feeding on each other as if they had been starving. His body fit against hers as if they were one.

Finally he loosened his arms and drew away to touch her hair, her wet cheek, her lips. He smiled and sighed.

"Was it that hard, Payne?" she whispered, her lips trembling. "They're just three little words: I love you."

He grinned, his teeth white against the color that was returning to his face. "I thought lightning might strike me, Hunter. I felt so sure you'd throw them back in my face." He sobered. "I couldn't have stood that."

"I'd never do that. They're too precious. Will I ever hear them again?"

"I love you. I love you very much, forever." He smiled again. "It gets easier. Do I have to tell you that you're the only woman who has ever heard that from me? Or ever will?" His love was warm in his black eyes.

"You'd better *not* be spreading those words around!" She wrapped her arms around him and pressed her face against his shirt, then looked up. "What's with this white shirt business? Are you going conservative on me?"

"I wanted to impress you."

"I'm impressed, but I don't know if I like it. I'd gotten used to all the paint smears and fringes. And the hat."

"I burned the hat," he said. "I told you I meant to change my ways, and that's a start. You said I hid behind it, so it's gone."

She frowned. "I'm not sure but that I'm going to miss it—not the hiding, but the hat. Don't get carried away with this reformation, okay?" She snuggled against him.

"Don't get too cozy there," he said. "I want you to look at that duplex with me."

"Now?" She pulled back to look at him. "Can't your investments wait?"

"It's not an investment, really. Or maybe it is, after all. I'm going to live in half and rent the other part. And it's not a duplex, actually. It's part of a planned community, very exclusive, with lots of green space and a great view of the mountains. Reasonably close to everything."

"You're going to live in it?" she asked, puzzled.

"Uh-huh. And you can rent the other half from me. Then you can have your own place, your privacy and your independence. That way you'll know

where to find me if I forget and run away again."
He grinned down at her. "I imagine we can come
to an agreement about how much rent you should
pay. If you get this fancy job, I'll raise your rent
and get rich."

"Fat chance," she said, laughing; "I'm not going
to let you get away with rent inflating." Her face
got serious as she thought about it.

He cupped her breast with one hand. "Of course,
you've got to expect the landlord to be lecherous."

"I certainly hope so." She sighed and took his
hand to kiss his fingers. "Lee? Do you really have
to sell the mountain house? If it's too unhandy in
the winter, we could close it and only use it in the
summer."

"I could be talked into anything. I didn't really
want to get rid of it." He kissed her neck. "But the
duplex will be a lot more convenient." He looked
into her face with his dark eyes. "The dividing
wall is only plasterboard. You could knock it down
all by yourself." He cleared his throat. "You'll have
to sign a lease, you know."

"Oh, really! For how long?"

"Forever?"

"That's pretty binding, isn't it?" She smiled happily at him.

"Very binding. In fact, the lease I have in mind
is more properly called a marriage license. I don't
want you to get away from me again." He kissed
her hair.

"Boy, you don't fool around do you, Payne?"

He drew back slightly to look at her seriously. "I
love you," he said, as if testing himself, then he
grinned impishly. "Hey, Hunter?"

She raised her eyebrows, blinking away tears.
"Hey, Payne, what?"

"You want to consummate the contract?"

Laughing softly, she reached for the knot in his tie. "There isn't anything I'd rather do. I thought you'd never get around to that."

THE EDITOR'S CORNER

We've received many compliments on the *LOVESWEPT* covers, particularly how original and innovative the "look" is. The overall design—that distinctive wave with veils of color on the front and back covers—came from the creative imagination of Bantam's Art Director, Leonard Leone. Len says the wave seemed a "natural" to him because the word *LOVESWEPT* immediately conjured up the image of that marvelous love scene on the beach in the movie, FROM HERE TO ETERNITY. He went on to line up the top—absolute top—cover painters in the business. And aren't the paintings exquisite? They seem to me to shimmer with tender sensuality. It's no wonder that Len Leone is known as the Dean of Art Directors in paperback publishing!

And inside the beautiful wrappings next month are still more delightful gifts for you. Joan J. Domning, whose first published work was the marvelously touching **HUNTER'S PAYNE** this month, is back in August with **TIGER LADY** (#13). It's set primarily in a computer company but—trust me!—you've never encountered a computer company like this one in a romance. I wouldn't want to spoil even one of Joan's charming surprises in this truly original love story, so I'm going to restrain myself from saying more. I'll just leave you with this tantalizing question: what would *you* do if the poetic man of your dreams spoke to you in gloriously romantic ways via a computer terminal . . . while the sensual, tender lover in your real life could scarcely speak to you?

(continued)

Iris Johansen's first romance came in "over the transom." That's publishing talk for a manuscript that is sent through the mail unagented and without a personal recommendation by another author or editor. Reading Iris's love story I could only say again and again "wow." I believe you, too, are going to say "wow" a lot when you read **STORMY VOWS** (#14). This is such a forceful, fast paced love story! In it, as in all Iris's romances (and you'll be reading lots of them in the months to come), the young and virginal heroine is swept into the realm of loving sensuality by the experienced and magnetic hero. But, nothing about **STORMY VOWS** or Iris's other love stories is the least bit old hat! They're just as fresh as winds whipping over the ocean. Now, *do* be sure to read **STORMY VOWS** very carefully and make a point of remembering all the characters. . . . Ah, sweet mystery! I simply can't resist a good surprise and there's a delightful one in this connection. I'll tell you all about it in the Editor's Corner next month.

Helen Mittermeyer specializes in romances in which the forceful hero is madly in love with and relentlessly pursues the skeptical heroine. You'll find twists on this specialty in Helen's marvelous love story **BRIEF DELIGHT** (#15). This romance is chockablock with surprising twists and breathless sexual tension. Part of the book is set in Saratoga Springs, New York, with its spas and baths, as well as the race track made famous by Edna Ferber in *Saratoga Trunk*. Some quaint and amusing characters wander through this delicious romance and help to further complicate the tempestuous love affair of the wonderfully matched heroine and hero!

The *LOVESWEPT* romances for August are real treats, but fair warning: they're only going to make those sultry summer days even more sultry! So I hope you'll be able to read them in the refreshing breezes along a beach or high on a mountain . . . or in air-conditioned comfort!

Carolyn Nichols

Carolyn Nichols
   Editor
LOVESWEPT
Bantam Books, Inc.
666 Fifth Avenue
New York, NY 10103

Love Stories you'll never forget by authors you'll always remember

☐	21603	**Heaven's Price** #1 Sandra Brown	$1.95
☐	21604	**Surrender** #2 Helen Mittermeyer	$1.95
☐	21600	**The Joining Stone** #3 Noelle Berry McCue	$1.95
☐	21601	**Silver Miracles** #4 Fayrene Preston	$1.95
☐	21605	**Matching Wits** #5 Carla Neggers	$1.95
☐	21606	**A Love for All Time** #6 Dorothy Garlock	$1.95
☐	21607	**A Tryst With Mr. Lincoln?** #7 Billie Green	$1.95
☐	21602	**Temptation's Sting** #8 Helen Conrad	$1.95
☐	21608	**December 32nd . . . And Always** #9 Marie Michael	$1.95
☐	21609	**Hard Drivin' Man** #10 Nancy Carlson	$1.95
☐	21610	**Beloved Intruder** #11 Noelle Berry McCue	$1.95
☐	21611	**Hunter's Payne** #12 Joan J. Domning	$1.95
☐	21618	**Tiger Lady** #13 Joan Domning	$1.95
☐	21613	**Stormy Vows** #14 Iris Johansen	$1.95
☐	21614	**Brief Delight** #15 Helen Mittermeyer	$1.95

Buy them at your local bookstore or use this handy coupon for ordering: